Alex

Necrotown

Mountain City Chronicles Book 1

By: Alexander Nader

Chapter 1

"This week is gonna suck for you." Fox trails a delicate hand across my throat. "You are going to die at least six times."

"Gee, thanks," I say. "Not exactly the kind of post-coital pillow talk I had in mind."

Fox balls up her hand and thumps a fist against my chest. "If you wanted delicate, you should have married a nymph. You wanted a badass, so you married me."

She's right.

When we met, I was in an alley, bleeding to death from matching eight-inch incisions up my forearms—clean cuts, too, no hesitation. I wanted to die. She gave me a reason to live.

"I love you," I tell her, wishing that conveyed anywhere near how much I felt about her.

"Good." She lies against my chest. Her red hair fans out and drapes across my body.

I kiss the top of her head and stare down the barrel of her silhouette. A fox tattoo is wrapped up in a ball on her hip.

Summertime in Mountain City means it's hot. Low rent living means the AC spits luke warm air—and that's on a good day. Therefore, my wife has all the covers kicked down to the foot of the bed, and I get an exclusive view of the most amazing curved hips I've ever seen.

"Don't you want to know?"

"Know what?" I reach over and grab a pack of cigarettes off the nightstand next to the bed.

"How you will die." Fox sees things. She's never told me if she's actually psychic or if she's just been alive so long she knows things; I've never asked.

That's part of the charm of our marriage; we've been through some shit in our long lives. When we got married last year we wrote our own vows. They were a pretty simple number: I promise to love and be faithful and never ask about any of the shit you pulled before this moment. So far, I think we are doing excellent.

"No, thanks," I say. "Let it be a mystery. C'est la vie, yeah?" I light up two cigarettes and pass one down to her.

"You're no fun sometimes." She pouts at me. Her lips look like heaven.

"Come on, life's gotta have at least a little mystery." I blow a smoke ring down at her.

"Like how to come up with enough money to pay the light bill?"

"Yeah, something like that."

"You know, Sam, you're a shit private eye."

"So why do you stay with me?" It's a joke, but sometimes I wonder. She's too perfect for me.

"Cause you're good in the sack." She grins and flicks her cigarette on my chest. Her finger traces lines in the ash. Down at her hip, the fox tattoo—Sune, yes, the tattoo has a name because it's a shithead—uncurls from its ball. Sune stretches and makes like she's digging her claws into Fox's side. The tattoo winks at me, curls back into a ball, and closes her eyes again.

3

"Can't argue there, I suppose." One last drag finishes off my cigarette, and I drop the butt in an empty whiskey bottle on the nightstand. "Ready to go again?"

"Easy, stud. I need a rest." Fox's red lashes blink closed as she gives me an evil wink.

Sune lifts her head up and rolls her eyes. The fox walks down Fox's hip and takes up a new home on the back of her calf. Like I said, the tattoo is a bit of a shit.

Three sharp knocks sound on the door. Strange. It's close to midnight, and I'm not expecting any company. My hand is barely closed around the grip of the revolver on the nightstand before Fox is halfway across the room. She creeps across the floor, naked except for the butcher knife in her right hand.

"Psst," I hiss at her. "Clothes?"

Fox glances down at herself, and then at the door.

"Be right there," I say, loud enough to be heard through the door. It doesn't take much. This far into the Glow landlords don't give much of a damn about soundproofing. Or much of anything else for that matter.

There's about three days' worth of laundry hanging out on our floor. I squint until I can make out a pair of jeans in the low light of the room. Jeans are great because they *tell* you not to wash them every time you wear them and generally don't get all wrinkly. Perfect for a guy who hates laundry. I kick the old pair of briefs out from inside the jeans and pull them on commando. Week-old denim? Sure. Twenty-four-hour-old crotch? Not so much.

By the time I can track down a shirt that smells only of tobacco, Fox is already dressed in a pair of sweat pants and a zip up cotton hoodie. I tuck the gun in the back of my jeans. Fox sees no need to hide the cleaver in her hand. Wouldn't matter if she did. I've seen Fox work—if she wants to cut you, she'll damn well cut you.

Alexander Nader

One more set of knocks at the door gives me a not-so-gentle reminder of the patience level of our guest. If only I gave a damn. I slow my gait so it takes a couple extra seconds to get to the door.

Seven deadbolts secure our small apartment. We don't have much, but addicts like to steal, and this slum is full of addicts. Drugs, drunks, fiends—you name it, the Glow is full of it. Worst part of town in one of the worst towns in the country. Well, second worst, but I don't want to talk about Necrotown.

As I'm unlatching the bolts, the energy in the air shifts—just a slight draw of energy tugging towards the door. Magic is always around, ready to be taken by the capable. Someone is ready and willing on the other side of the door. I close my free hand around the grip of the 357 snub nose tucked into my pants. I trust Mages as little as I trust the Standards. The bolts clunk and thunk as I unlatch them, and I swear the guest huffs. I swing open the door just as another set of knocks rattle off.

"Can I help you?" I ask in the gritted-teeth accent of someone about to evict a persistent Jehovah's Witness.

"I have my doubts, but I have no one else to turn to," the old man standing at the door says.

"Well, if it isn't my old friend, Lloyd Burgess." I open the door to admit the old man, who is anything but my friend.

Burgess attempts to smile at me, but it comes off as a sneer. Or maybe it was meant to be a sneer from the start. I turn my back to him and search my desk for something to drink; I'm going to need it.

The empty glasses clatter together, but that's all they are, empty glasses. I settle for a smoke. As I light it up, I lean against the wall and turn my attention back to Burgess.

To my side, Fox grips her knife tight. Sune is on the side of Fox's neck, teeth barred. The growl would be audible if tattoos could make sound, but that would be ridiculous.

Necrotown: Mountain City Chronicles

"What do you want, Burgess?" I run my foot over the carpet, snagging my toes on loose pieces of shag left over from the disco era.

"I want to hire a private eye." Burgess plants his cane and leans forward on it with both hands. The solid gold handle is encrusted with more jewels than the Queen of bloody England.

"And?"

Burgess smiles. The gesture is genuine this time. I think the old bastard enjoys these games. Men with more money than god must entertain themselves somehow, I suppose.

"You've worked for me before, and it worked out so well. I had another job and thought you to be just the man." The cane creaks against my floor as he leans further forward.

"Lucrative for you. Do you know how many times that deal has gotten me killed? Three. Three times. I've had my neck broken because of you and your jobs *three times*." I should kick that cane right out from underneath him.

Fox shoots a questioning glance my way, but I shake my head. We don't ask questions, and I damn sure don't want to talk about Lloyd Burgess and his jobs.

"I made sure you were rightly compensated for the work you did." Burgess scans my apartment. His forehead creases and liver spots get swallowed up by crater-sized wrinkles. "You clearly didn't put the money to any form of use. Stashing cash from the missus?"

"Fuck you, old man." Fox takes a step.

Burgess holds up a hand. "I meant no disrespect. Let me make it up to you."

"No." I'm done with this.

"I pay considerably well, this job even more so than the last one."

"No."

"I'll triple your salary from the weapons job."

I sigh. He's talking some big numbers, and if anyone could back it up, it would be Lloyd Burgess. He's the only guy in Mountain City rich enough to pull off wearing an ascot. Plus, he's got influence. I didn't think to take advantage of that the first time around, but he could help with a mystery that's been bothering me for a few decades. "What's the job?"

"My daughter has gone missing."

"Kidnapped or run away?" Fox rests the cleaver against the outside of her leg. Apparently, she doesn't consider Burgess an immediate threat. Then again, if she had, he would be dead already.

"Brainwashed into running away. She's been hanging around with the filth down in Necrotown. I think she may be residing in that cesspool."

Necrotown is home of the Necros. Necros happen to be death Mages. Lucky for the whole world, they are generally terrible at it and can't do much more than make a dead frog twitch. If they ever figure out how to harness their power, though, the rest of the world could be screwed.

"Why us? Why him?" Fox points the meat cleaver at me. "Don't look at me like that, he may be my husband, but he's a terrible private eye in the worst part of town. Now, I'm sure there are plenty of overqualified dicks downtown who would love to have this job."

Fox walks to the window and back. In the city skyline, the lights of Burgess's tower shine like the North Star—a guiding beacon for all looking to make money.

"You are correct. However, for all the qualifications they do have, they are lacking one important function."

Fox's eyebrows arch in question.

"Discretion. The last thing I need is news of my daughter prancing around in that cesspool to hit the papers."

"Especially not with all your Pro-Standard family values campaigns going," I say.

Mountain City is full of different races, none of them more annoying than the Standards. Normal humans who think their mean mugs'll melt you with a harsh stare. They generally have inferiority complexes that could make Napoleon Bonaparte blush. Most of the other inhabitants of Mountain City can tear them apart. None more so than Burgess's arch enemies, the Hairs. He's been trying to get them evicted from the city for as long as I can remember.

Burgess takes a deep breath. That one may have hit close to home for him, but ever the politician, he plays it straight. "One of the many reasons, I assure you."

"So you want Sam to find your daughter and keep his mouth shut?" Fox paces to the corner of the apartment that serves as our kitchen and back to the window.

"Precisely," Burgess says. The smug old man thinks money can buy him anything. "You obviously need the money, and after our previous venture, I am sure of your husband's trustworthiness."

"Shove off," I say. "I'm done working for you."

Burgess sticks a hand in his pocket, takes out a piece of paper. He sets the small rectangle on my kitchen table/office desk/laundry folding station, careful not to actually touch anything with his hands as he does so.

"Consider this a retainer for your services. I'll pay triple your normal daily rate, plus expenses. When this check is cashed, I'll know you have made your decision, but please hurry. I need my daughter back. Her name is Sarah Roswell, and if you get her back to me quietly, I'll make this check look like pennies." Burgess taps his fingers against the piece of paper.

"Roswell?"

"Yes." Burgess bristles, like a chill just ran up his back. Not annoyance, I'd swear it's fear but that doesn't fit right. "She goes by her mother's maiden name as tribute to my late wife. Mrs. Roswell passed away quite some time ago."

"So there's no blood in the water between you two?" Fox measures Burgess up, all feminine scrutiny and distrust. Smart woman. "When we find her she's not gonna tell us she ran away because you laid your filthy hands on her, right?"

If Burgess was afraid, it's gone. Rage dissolves whatever the mystery emotion was. He snatches a pair of leather gloves out of his pocket and fights to stretch them over his boney fingers. "Mr. Flint, I trust you will do the right thing and find my daughter." Burgess is speaking to me, but his predatory glare is focused solely on Fox. "In the meantime, it would be in your best interest to keep that," Burgess points two black leather fingers at Fox's chest like a gun, "in check before she gets you both hurt."

"Fuck you, old man. Get out of my house." Fox stomps toward Burgess, but he's out the door before she gets there. With Burgess's exit, the residual magical energy flows back into the room. My bet is Burgess had a bodyguard hanging out in the hallway somewhere. Mages make good mercs and bodyguards.

"What the hell was that?" Fox slams the cleaver into the chopping block on the kitchen counter, burying the blade two inches deep in the bamboo.

"Exactly what it was."

"So you've done jobs for Burgess before?"

"Yeah." I think about the last time I got my neck snapped because of Burgess' job. A pain wells up at the base of my skull, and I rotate my head around to get rid of it.

Fox knows I'm done talking; she won't push. What's done is done, ashes to ashes and all that jazz. Instead, she moves to the kitchen table. "Does that old sack of puss think he can buy us off just like that? Sounds like he royally screwed you with that other job."

"Yes, he can buy us off, and yeah, I made a couple enemies working for him. At least this is something totally different. Besides, he's connected. Maybe he can help me find out about my parents."

Forty years ago, my parents went missing. They went out one night and never came back. Cops didn't do shit for an investigation, but that's not surprising. The Standards never look out for anyone but their own.

"Your parents have been gone a long time," Fox says. Her voice is soothing. She knows that losing my parents hit me hard.

It's not like I was some kind of momma's boy, but I've been alive a long time and my parents were the one constant in a changing world. Them disappearing set me on the downward spiral Fox saved me from.

"They've only been gone forty years," I say. "That's not *that* long. Not for us anyway."

Fox watches me closely, but doesn't say anything. She's been alive long enough to know that years don't count the same for us.

"You know once, my dad forgot their anniversary?" I laugh at the memory. "Mom was so pissed she walked out and didn't come back for two years. Dad said it was the quietest two years of his life."

A sad smile touches Fox's lips. "Whatever you want to do, I support you. I know how much your parents meant to you, but you know this job means a trip to Necrotown? You hate it down there."

"No, I hate the Glow. Necrotown just gives me the creeps."

"Either way, you think this check and the *possiblility* Burgess might help with your parents are enough to make you get over your fear?" Fox sets her hand on the paper, waiting for my answer, I suppose.

"I'm sure it is. Anything would be enough, but that guy's got more than anything. He's got everything."

Fox flips the check over. Sune scrambles across her arm and down to Fox's wrist to see it. Fox's mouth drops open, and I swear I can hear Sune whistle in amazement. That could just have been Fox's breath catching in her chest though.

"That's a lot of money," she says when she returns to a normal breathing pattern. She still puts one hand on the back of our wooden chair to steady herself.

I pull out the metal chair next to her and take a seat. There's a pack of smokes on the table, and I light up a pair. A drink would be tops right now, but apparently we live in a dry household at the moment. Burgess's check will see to filling the wells. "You think liquor stores cash checks?"

Fox passes me the check. "Probably not ten thousand dollar checks."

There it is. One rectangle with a business font and black business cursive represents more money than I've seen this year. Looks like I'm on a missing person's case.

"No, but I bet Walmart does."

"Like I want to give those Standard bastards any more money than I already do."

Standards own everything, hands down. Anything that doesn't belong to them is because none of them want it. The government has to do something to make them feel equal or whatever, so there's all kinds of Standard grants and subsidies set up to help them start businesses. Mages, Hairs, and all the other weirdos like us get all the "power," and the Standards get all the money. Bullshit.

11

Necrotown: Mountain City Chronicles

Fox takes the spare cigarette out of my hand. Ten grand made me forget about it as the pile of ash on the kitchen table attests. She puffs on the stick with lips still stained red from the night's ruby lipstick, long since smeared away but never quite gone. Sune rests with her head on Fox's shoulder, watching me intently.

"I suppose this can wait for the morning." I set the check back on the table, careful to keep it away from the lighter and ashtray. Somehow I don't see Burgess being big on reprinting checks. One last pull, and I'm down to the filter.

How in the hell am I stuck working for Lloyd Burgess again? I think about how big a mess the last job turned out to be.

"Hey." Fox lifts my chin with her index finger until I'm staring into her blue eyes. The intensity in her gaze burns with a passion only she can have. This body suits her well. "Looks like you've got a lot on your mind."

"Sorry." I flip my extinguished butt at the kitchen sink. It bounces off a pizza pan, crusted with burnt cheese, and drops into an old glass of brown water. The city never has given much of a shit about water quality this far south.

"Well, clearly you're thinking about something other than me, and that's your problem." Fox unzips her hoodie, unveiling an hourglass of milky smooth skin.

Suddenly, I no longer give a shit about Burgess, his daughter, or the last job—or how many lives I have left. The only thing in my brain is her body and how I could use a drink. The drink can wait, she can't.

Chapter 2

I wake up late the next afternoon with the chills. Fox moans and a smile touches her lips as I slide out from under her to check the thermostat. The thing says it's 78 in here. Then why the hell am I shivering? I hold my hand out and it trembles. Just in need of some caffeine, I'm sure.

The tiny coffee pot is buried behind six mismatched coffee cups, two plates with pizza crumbs, and a dead plant. How a coffee pot that gets used daily ends up behind a plant, I'll never know. These questions aren't to be answered, just mysteries like where all the damn socks go and why servers only ask how your meal is when you have a mouthful of cheeseburger.

Brewing coffee quietly is a science. I am not a scientist; I pour the last of the coffee grinds in without measuring and bang the carafe off at least six different fixtures before I get the water poured into the top. I click on the pot and head for a quick shower.

Lukewarm water in this weather leaves me feeling slightly more gross than when I got in. A healthy dose of cologne and deodorant leave me feeling fresher and clean enough to find Burgess's daughter. After coffee. And whiskey. I'll definitely be ready after coffee and whiskey. The tremor in my hands has died down to more of a buzz, but my body hurts. I swear, dying doesn't hurt near as much as living.

Fox is propped up against the headboard of the bed, drinking coffee out of one of last night's wine glasses. She yawns and covers her mouth with the back of her hand. "Thanks for the coffee." She salutes me with her glass. "But we really need some bacon."

"I checked earlier. The fridge is empty."

"Ten thousand bucks will fix that though. We need to get that in the bank so you can take me somewhere nice to eat. Trim that goatee and put on your good blue jeans, you're taking this lady to the Steakery tonight."

Necrotown: Mountain City Chronicles

Sune is on Fox's wrist, sniffing at the coffee. The animal tattoo licks her teeth at the mention of steak. Even my stomach growls.

"I've got to get this check cashed first and grab a little pick me up. So let's hit the road." I make my way to the coffee pot and find a splash left in the bottom. There aren't any clean cups in the vicinity so I drink straight from the pot.

"Hit the road? How long have we been married, Mr. Flint? Do you know how much dolling up I have to do for a trip to the best steakhouse in Mountain City? You go ahead and run to the bank and the store while I get ready." Fox drains the last of her cup. "And pick up some coffee. I was going to make you some, but we're out of grounds."

"Thanks for thinking of me."

"I forgot about your needs for my own." Fox kicks out from under the covers and makes for the bathroom. "Now get going, you have a dinner to take me to."

"Yes, ma'am." I make a move like I'm tipping a hat.

She blows me a kiss and disappears into the shower.

I grab a clean pair of boxers and slide back into last night's jeans. With a little luck, I find a clean long-sleeve shirt and a vest. I'm not exactly in with current style, but some styles just stuck with me. A pair of tan, steel-toe boots and my trusty revolver finishes my going-out clothes. I'm ready for my day. Two steps down the hallway, I remember the check, still sitting on the kitchen table.

When I get back in the apartment, the sound of water running comes from the bathroom. The thought of Fox, naked and wet comes to mind and I have to fight all kinds of primal urges to grab the check and head back out the door. The rent is overdue, after all.

The walls of the hallway are spray-painted with various signs and sigils. A healing crest here and a protection ward there—simple magic might protect someone from a Standard but wouldn't do much to anything else. Still, peace of mind is peace of mind, and in the ghetto, you can never have enough.

The rest of the graffiti is various race signs. Hairs, Sharps, Stones—whatever, they are all just kids looking to mark their territory, and, except for the executive offices downtown, the Glow is really the only place where the races overlap.

We are kind of like a redneck version of the five burrows. See, they've got the right idea up in New York. The Standards get Manhattan, Mages run Brooklyn, the Hairs own the Bronx, Sharps are stashed away on Staten Island, and the Stones party hard in Queens.

I like the separation, though, it keeps things simple. If a Hair wanders into Sharp territory and finds himself someone's dinner, he had that shit coming. That's how we do it anyway. Not like fucking Hollywood where everyone is all over each other—Trolls and Mages sharing housing, Hairs serving Standards at restaurants, all for what? A chance to hit it big on the silver screen? Everyone thinks they are the next big star, but they aren't.

Around here, everyone knows to stay in their burrow and everything will be fine. Mountain City is divided up the same as New York, just without the hip street names. The middle of the city is Downtown. Business district is good for everyone, neutral ground. Then, starting in the Northwest and going clockwise you have Standards, Trolls, Hairs, Sharps, The Glow, and then the Mages, bringing you back around to the Standards. The Glow is like Downtown because it's open to anyone, but different by fewer zeroes on the ends of the citizens' bank accounts.

The front door of the apartment building used to be glass. Now it's just a frame, a steel rectangle good for little more than getting in the way. I duck under it and step out onto the sidewalk. Two small wolf cubs chase each other through the door and inside, almost knocking me over in the process. Their yipping echoes down the hall as they play. Good to know someone's having fun.

Necrotown: Mountain City Chronicles

The Glow gets its name from all the neon. The evening is still young, and the only lights on now are the ones that shop owners are too lazy to bother turning off during the day, but at night this place lights up like a thousand red-light districts. Sure, we've got those too, but there's more here—magic supply shops, Herbalistas, fortune tellers, bowling alleys. The Glow has it all.

I hate it here.

One of these days I'm moving Fox and I out of this godforsaken place. Maybe if Burgess comes through on his promises, I'll finally be able to afford to do that.

Not likely.

There's one bank in all of the Glow. "Bank" is an overstatement, more like cash advance store because that's all anyone ever gets out of the place. If you do business down here, you do it in cash. The few people that have gainful employment to the North all use the bank to cash their checks and then live off the green. I'd be surprised if anyone other than me even has an account.

I walk the three blocks to the bank and step inside. The bank tellers all sit behind bulletproof glass. I doubt anyone other than well-trained Mages can see it, but there are magic seals on the glass, stopping any kind of foul play. This is a Standard-owned bank, and they aren't taking any chances on one of us knocking over their thriving business every time we need a fix.

One teller doesn't have a customer, and I step up to his window. "Hello, can I cash this, please?"

The teller clicks around on his computer. From the reflection in his plastic-rimmed glasses, I can see he's browsing the internet. I take a deep breath and wait patiently. My hand drums against the counter.

Eventually, the teller decides to talk. "Can I help you?"

"Yes," I say. "I'd like to cash this, please." I slide the check into a metal drawer at the front of the desk.

The teller doesn't take his eyes off the screen as he reaches in the drawer and withdraws the check. He glances down and then decides I'm worthy of his attention. The guy looks me up and down two dozen times. "I'm sorry, sir. My computer is locked up, I've got to go check with..." His voice trails off as he gets up and leaves his station.

At least he attempted some tact, I suppose. I know he's just going to the back to call Burgess and make sure I didn't rip him off somehow. Can't blame the teller. One look at my account and he can see I've never put a check that big in before.

"It's ridiculous. They are lies that have just perpetuated more lies." The voice comes from the TV in the lobby I hadn't noticed on my way in.

The caption on the screen reads, "Hair representative claims violence spurred by Standards." The guy on the screen is Ethan Grisom, Hair Alpha male extraordinaire. I don't care for the guy, personally, but I've seen the way the Hairs get treated. My old friend Burgess has been waging a smear campaign on them for a long time.

"And why should we listen to you?" a Standard says from across the table. "Your own father murdered one of our prominent citizens. The beast tore the poor woman to pieces, and now you're here, just like always, claiming the pacifism of your people. We just don't buy it. Everyone knows how the Hairs make their money; you can't tell us you aren't violent when you deal guns for a living."

Even in his human form, Ethan's hackles raise. His golden eyes glow for a minute before he takes a deep breath. He runs a hand through his black hair and scratches at a patch of gray in his beard. The rumors all say Hairs have trigger tempers, but even as little as I like Ethan, I've got to admit he keeps his cool. Well, most of the time anyway.

"My father didn't commit that crime. The court case was a sham, and the evidence circumstantial at best. The Standards just needed a scapegoat to explain the grisly murder of one of their own.

17

It could have just as easily been one of the Sharps or even another Standard."

The talk show host opens his mouth, but Ethan talks over him. "And, yes, guns are the Hair's industry. Everyone knows that. All of our dealings are completely up front and legal. We pay taxes on all of our sales."

"But—"

"We have a business license. We run background checks before selling guns to people."

"Yes, well wha—"

"I refuse to sell armor piercing or explosive rounds as a courtesy to the Mountain City PD."

The host keeps talking, but Ethan's thick growl of a voice drowns him out. Ethan finishes his rant just in time for the host to say, "...advice from a madman's son. You are probably out of your mind like your father." The host's face burns red with conviction. He's out of breath from trying to talk over the Alpha.

I expect Ethan to flip out right there. Swap hands for claws, beard for fur, and tear into the asshole. The guy probably deserves it, but no. Ethan smiles. His eyes glow golden again, but this time it's with amusement.

"Every day my company sells close to one thousand firearms. Business is up ten percent over last year, and we have shown steady growth since I took over the company twenty years ago. The number one reason my clients list for purchasing firearms is protection. Number two? Personal amusement," he goes on.

"I can tell you exactly how many pistols I sell in a given day. I can show you a graph of shotgun spread patterns. Give me ten minutes, and I'll show you how to break down any gun to nothing more than a handful of parts."

The host smiles, like he thinks Ethan is making himself look crazy, spewing out numbers. "Yes, but these are just sales figures. Any good executive knows a few stats."

"But the most important statistic of all? Ninety-eight percent of all of our sales are to Standards."

The host swallows.

"Second most important statistic? The number of cases of a Hair attacking a human resulting in fatality. In the past thirty years, the answer is one. The number of Hair lives taken by Standard firearms? Twenty-six."

"Well, you can't—"

"Twenty-six a year," Ethan says. "So you see, I am selling you the guns to kill my own people. I'm sure you can guess how that makes me feel. And yes, you are absolutely right, Mr. O'Malley, I'm in a rotten business—a business made rotten by the Standards that enable it."

The show cuts to commercial break as the stammering host flips through a handful of papers in his lap, looking for the BS statistic to turn things around on the Alpha.

"He's hot," a woman waiting at the window next to me says to her friend. They both giggle like schoolgirls and lean their heads in closer to talk further about Mr. Sex Symbol.

"Sorry about your wait, sir." My teller returns to clicking away at his computer.

"No problem."

"Would you like any cash back?"

"I would like it all back in cash."

The teller does a double take before punching away at his computer some more. "I'm afraid I can't give it all back. Your account is $1,293.82 in the negative. I can't cash the check with your account not in balance."

"Why don't you take $1,300 out of that check right there to set my account right and then give me the leftover $8,700? Sounds like a pretty fair deal, don't it?" My shaking hand rattles against the metal tray under the glass.

The teller looks at my shakes, his lip curled. He beats up his keyboard a little more before asking if there's any particular way I would like my money back.

"Big bills." I hate having a pocket full of money, but no matter where you go, cash talks. I need that if I'm going to figure out anything about Sarah Roswell and how to get her home.

The guy counts out eighty-seven hundred-dollar bills and passes them to me through the tray along with a receipt for my deposit.

"Thank you." I fold the cash in half and tuck it in my back pocket.

As I turn, the teller next to mine leans over. "Can you believe those two dumb bimbos fawning over that disgusting Hair?" She speaks in a whisper that can be heard across the whole lobby. The two girls are already gone.

Standard and Hair relations haven't been the best. The case they were talking about with Ethan's dad? The dead lady was Eleanor Roswell, Lloyd Burgess's wife. Burgess has been on a one man "destroy the Hairs" campaign ever since then. When the case first broke, people were skeptical, it didn't seem to fit. A spectacle of a court case ended with Ethan's dad on his way to the injection chamber and a whole city full of whispers. Those whispers have been getting louder and louder for years now.

There were all kinds of weird details about the case, but I was distracted at the time and didn't pay much attention. People I trust say it was a setup, that Papa Grisom didn't do it. That's about all I can say.

Outside the bank, the Glow's stank air is a welcome relief from the stuffy death of the bank. Magic fills the air down here, and it tastes like a sweaty melting pot. There's a steady hum, like standing too close to a live power line. Well, real Mages might feel that way. For me, it's more like licking a battery—just a slight tingle. I try not to focus on the taste though. Magic is not my strong suit; I'm not a Mage, and it's best to leave matters of sorcery to the sorcerers.

Even better, I now have cash for liquor. And, of course, a steak dinner, but mostly the whiskey. My body gets warm just thinking about it. The liquor store is only a block east of the bank.

Espozino's Sewage Wine and Fine Liquor glows with neon allure, even before dusk. Alcoholics buzz in and out of the place like a hive. Laborers with shit jobs grab a quick pick-me-up before their shift starts. Schmucks in fancy suits swing in for a bottle to serve as their night cap, wine for the wife, fuzzy navel mixers for the mistress.

I'm simple, just a quick fifth to split with Fox, and I'm set. Well, a sixty-forty split anyway. Hell, who am I kidding? I've got enough cash to pick up a bottle each. I whistle as I swing open the glass door covered in warnings and ads: Bartlet's Whiskey guaranteed to put hair on your chest; No one under fifteen admitted without a $100 "tip;" Schnelligan's Wine will get you laid; We no longer carry Zebox Diet Cosmo Mix as it's been found to cause cases of violent death; and so on.

The owner—a guy with a mustache to make Captain Hook jealous, garter belts around the biceps of his dress shirt, and tattoos creeping out from under the collar—nods as I step in. "How's it go today, Sam?"

"I'm getting along. How about you, Warsaw?"

Necrotown: Mountain City Chronicles

For a Standard, Warsaw's not such a bad guy. He always gives me a discount on my bottles and has never given me a reason to not shop here. The Glow is three square miles of poverty, and as such, there are at least four different package stores in the Glow alone. Warsaw's is the best of the four and the closest to my house.

"Pretty fine." Warsaw bags a bottle of Queen's Gambit Cognac and takes two tens from the customer in exchange. One bill goes in the drawer, one in Warsaw's pocket—owner of the store gets to decide what sales get posted. Taxes on liquor are a real son-of-a-bitch. Taxes on everything, as a matter of fact, fall into the son-of-a-bitch category.

"Say, mate, you havin' your usual bottle of well rocket fuel?" Warsaw already has the bottle out from under the counter.

Noxius Special Reserve Oil Barrel Aged Whiskey is the cheapest shit you can buy. Plastic bottle with a plastic cap. The liquor is so shitty, it's a wonder the stuff doesn't eat through the bottle by the time anyone gets around to drinking it. Most people don't survive for a second bottle. I have developed a fond place in my heart for it.

"Not today, Saw." I slap the counter. "I'm having a fine day, and I need two bottles of something fine to celebrate it with."

Warsaw cocks an eyebrow. "Really?"

"Really."

The liquor-keep shrugs and snatches a set of keys off the desk. He turns to unlock a cabinet behind the counter.

"Whoa, whoa, whoa, good sir. I said something to celebrate with, not something to woo the president with. Holy shit, man. I don't go from choking down seventeen cent swill to thousand dollar a bottle rapper drink overnight."

"You said 'something fine,' I though you meant 'something fine.'" Warsaw slaps the keys back down on the desk.

"Well, when I said 'something fine' let's just assume I meant 'something finer than Ol' Noxius,' deal?"

Warsaw cocks his fist back for a second before forcing his hand to open, grabs a bottle of Kerrigan Irish Whiskey, and sets it on the counter. "How's this?"

"Will fifty bucks buy me two of them?"

"Two and a free bottle of seltzer."

"SOLD!" I slap my cash on the counter.

"No, no, man, you're the fucking best, bruh." The voices carry through the glass even before the doors slide open to admit four Stones. The group of rock heads sprint in different directions and start grabbing bottles like overgrown kids in a candy store.

"Fucking Stones, yeah?" Warsaw says as he bags my bottles.

Stones are what some people would call Gargoyles, and they tend to be annoying as all hell.

"I wish they would just calm down." Warsaw slides the bag over to me, while trying to keep his eyes on all four of the bros in his store.

Glass shatters. "Shit. Sorry. Sorry. I'll pay for that."

"Fucking right yeh will," Warsaw shouts back. He opens the drawer and puts my bill inside, withdrawing a fifty dollar bill for change and an extra twenty to go in his pocket. One of these days the IRS is going to eat his ass alive.

"I noticed that was quite the stack of bills you had there, mate. You hit the lottery, yeah?"

"Shhh," I say. "It's dangerous out there." I glance out the windows and give a fake shudder.

"Yeah, 'dangerous,' says the man who lives forevah."

"It's called Quasi-Immortal for a reason, Saw. Cats only get nine lives, you know? One of these days, I'll run out." I scoop up the bottles in my arm like an infant. Probably be equally as nurturing of my hangover tomorrow.

"How many lives you used, Flint?"

"Too many." Always too many.

"Hey, barkeep, have you got any Dan Perrywinkle back there?" A Stone in a pink polo shirt with the collar popped up elbows me to the side so he can lean on the counter.

The whiskey bottles in my bag clank together as I stumble. I'd consider punching the dumb ass in the jaw, but even in fleshy-human mode, the guy's still thick as a skyscraper beam. The satisfaction isn't worth the broken knuckles.

"Take it fuckin' easy, yeah." Warsaw puts his hands up to the Stone and glances at me.

I give him the 'yeah, I'm outta here' nod and start for the door with my new friend Kerrigan.

"Yeah, I got Perrywinkle," I hear Saw say. "Have you got the cash for that sort of thing?"

Over my shoulder I catch a glimpse of the Stone. He runs a hand across a stalactite stiff, faux-hawk and snatches a wad of cash out of his pocket. "Yeah, bruh, I got the cash."

The other three Stones meet up with their buddy at the register. I could hang around to hurry the rock-heads out and save Warsaw the trouble, but eh, he can handle himself.

"Man, this party is gonna be sweet, dude," faux-hawk hair says.

"No shit. I've never partied down in N-Town before."

Fuck.

Did they have to mention Necrotown? As a private eye, I should ask them what's up, but the only thing worse than talking to Stones is Necrotown. Seeing as how Burgess is sponsoring today's bout of alcoholism...

"Excuse me," I step back to the counter. "What's going on in Necrotown?"

Pink polo Stone turns from the counter and takes me in. He half-chuckles, and the sound comes more from his chest than anywhere else. "Yeah, mister, there's a big bonanza going on down south."

Another bro in shorts and boat shoes slaps Pink Polo on the back. "It's gonna be so fucking hype, man."

"What's the occasion?" I ask. "It's been a while since I've been down that way, might be worth a look."

All four Stones look at me, suddenly suspicious. As if I'm a cop. As if the cops give a single shit about what goes on down in Necrotown.

I reach into my pocket and take out a fifty. "First bottle's on me tonight, boys."

Boat Shoes snatches up the bill. "Sweet. Now I don't have to borrow money for a bottle. The big man down south, Bumba Master, or whatever—"

"It's Blade Master, you fucking idiot," Pink Polo corrects.

"Bloodmonger, technically," I say.

He's the head honcho down in Necrotown. The guy is as talented a Mage as a rock is talented at flight school. Either way, there's no point in correcting the Stones.

25

"Yeah, sure. Blade Master is throwing some big party over a girl. I think he's getting married or some shit. They're saying it's going to be the party of the century, bro."

Another Stone slaps himself and howls like he's some sort of Hair or something. Howler and Boat Shoes jump and bump chests. I puke in my throat a little bit.

"Yeeaaahhh," the both of them scream and go to bump chests again.

Mid-air, Boat Shoes grunts and his muscles freeze. He hits the ground stuck in his chest-out pose and falls to his side. Gray streaks run down his arms, painting his body the color of stone. The granite version of the Stone rests on the ground, frozen mid-chest bump.

"Jesus fucking Christ," Warsaw says. "Pay for your bloody drinks, and get him the 'ell outta here. Can't have one of you rock-heads clogging up my store. We got enough decorations as it is."

"Ah, shit," Pink Polo says. "Man, Tucker's gone hard. Last time, he was hard thirty-six hours. He's going to miss the party."

"Bummer," the other three mutter in unison.

Tricky thing about the Stones, they never know when they are going to turn to rock. Randomly they turn, and no one knows how long they will stay that way. There have been rumors of Stones staying frozen for years, decades even. That's why they are all carpe diem, 'seize the moment' assholes—at any moment they could freeze for the rest of their lives, and they don't want to miss the party.

"Fucking really?" Warsaw shouts as the three Stones shove past me out the front door.

"Can you believe this?" The liquor-slinger comes out from behind the counter to examine Boat Shoes, frozen solid in front of the counter.

"Stones are about good for nothing, man."

"Care to give me a hand with this?" he says.

I sigh and set my bottles on a bench by the door. No need to mess up my vest so I slide out of it and set it on top of my Kerrigan.

Warsaw grabs a dolly out from under a stack of Zero vodka cases and brings it around behind the Stone. "I can't believe you wear a peacoat and vest year round. You really are going for that Dorian Gray look, yeah?"

"Shut up, Saw." I grab the Stone around the neck and lean it forward. The thing weighs a damn ton, and I can't help but grunt as I try not to drop the kid. "You look like you belong in a soda shop quartet."

Warsaw slides the bottom of the dolly under the feet of the gargoyle. "Touché."

I let the Stone down and shove it back. Warsaw leans the dolly back and pushes it out the front door. There is a jewelry shop next door to the liquor store—the place carries the kind of accessories you can get out of a vending machine since it gets robbed about once a day. Warsaw parks Boat Shoes right next to the door, slides his dolly free, and heads back inside.

"There. Someone else's problem now, yeah?"

"You're a great neighbor, sir. Remind me never to move my practice next door." My coat and drinks sit on the bench where I left them. I scoop them all up in my arms.

"As if you could afford the rent. You can barely keep the lights on in your roach motel, mate."

I shrug. "At least I make enough to keep the drink flowing."

"Good point. You can't afford your rent, but at least you're paying mine. Have a good one, Nine Lives. Try to keep above ground, yeah?"

"Yeah."

If what Fox said is true, I might not be spending much time above ground this week. Doesn't much matter, though. I'll come back, or I won't.

And so it goes.

I exit through the front and contemplate the bottles tucked under my jacket. These could make for a good afternoon at home with Fox. Whatever shindig Bloodmonger has planned, it surely won't start until after dark. Necros are predictable like that. Death and dark and fire and blood and bullshit chanting. Not to mention their magic tastes like dirt.

That gives me plenty of time to get drunk and lose myself in Fox and still be somewhat sober in time to make my way down to Necrotown.

Lost in my thoughts, I bump into a concrete barrier.

"Sam Flint, good to see you," the barrier says.

Correction. It's not a block of concrete, it's a Troll. Trolls are exactly what they sound like, big and dumb. And loan sharks. There are two places to get money in Mountain City, Standards and Trolls. It's a widely accepted conspiracy theory that the Standards finance the Trolls. Trolls are the easiest race to manipulate. The Standards can control the flow of money to every other race through the Trolls. The setup is genius. Burgess is probably the one who came up with it.

Regardless of where the money originally came from, the Trolls are the ones who loaned some to me a while back, and now I owe them. Yeah, yeah, I know, a Quasi-Immortal shouldn't be in debt to some lumbering oafs, but what can I say? I'm a big spender.

"Hey, Brutus," I say. Yes, the Troll's name is Brutus. No, I don't want to get into just how very predictable that is.

"You are hard man to find," Brutus says. He opens and closes his hands a few times, knuckles popping loud as firecrackers.

"Oh, you know, I've been here and there."

"I think you have been hiding. You are late."

That's got a lot to do with why I'm hard to find. "Nah, Brutus, that has nothing to do with it. I've just been, you know, busy. But I just got a new job, and I'll be able to pay you back soon."

I don't see the punch coming. It must be some kind of looping right hook because it connects behind my left ear. I put all this together as I'm coming to my senses on the ground. With one hand on the pavement, I try to push back to my feet. A size eighteen boot crunches the fingers of my left hand. They literally crunch. The scream that wrenches itself from my throat is automatic.

Brutus leans down and covers my mouth with a hand. People walking by on the sidewalk give us a wide berth. Down in the Glow this is a regular occurrence. The Trolls have a tendency to beat payments out of people.

"You will pay now and later." The Troll grabs one of my whiskey bottles off the pavement. He shatters the bottle across the top of my head. The shot is well placed; it doesn't steal my consciousness like the first shot. He wants me to feel this, and trust me, I do.

Brutus reaches into my pocket and steals my wad of Burgess' money. All I can think about how much the whiskey burns in the cut the bottle made on my forehead. The Troll kicks me in the ribs. The two lowest crack. I suck in a breath and get a few drops of whiskey that have been leaking down my face. This sends me into a coughing fit. The coughing with broken ribs is like getting a massage from Edward Scissorhands.

"I get the point," I spit out between coughs.

"No, you don't," Brutus says. He picks up the other whiskey bottle. Head, more ribs, head, I manage to block a couple shots with my elbows, but one heavy blow shatters the bottle against my already broken lower ribs. The fight in me is officially gone. I give up and wait for him to beat me to death. I'll die, and be reborn and fixed.

Brutus roughs me up a little more and leaves me in a pile of blood and whiskey on the sidewalk. "Not that easy, immortal."

Fuck. Credit where credit's due; the Trolls sure know how to make a point.

"Officer," the Troll shouts. His voice echoes down the sidewalk.

A man in blue comes my way. How the Troll managed to have a cop around, I'll never know. Police in the Glow are as rare as Trolls with a conscience.

"The drunk just took a swing at me. I wasn't trying to hurt him none, but he just wouldn't leave me be." The Troll leaves me with Mr. Policeman. I try to babble an explanation, but concussion and battered body has me babbling like a drunk. The officer is at least kind enough to pick up my vest and drape it over my cuffs after he arrests me. A real gentleman, that cop.

Chapter 3

Jails in Mountain City, or any city for that matter, are an impressive feat. Standards, Mages, Hairs, Trolls, and all sorts of other delinquents spend time in lockup, so the jail systems have to be prepared to house all sorts of nuisance. All cells get caged in with bars of iron and floors of limestone. The iron cancels out low-level magic, and limestone acts as an insulator against the power in the air. Any magic on the outside of the jail stays there.

I'm no expert at magic. Even if I was, there wouldn't be shit I could do about the cell I'm stuck in. The bars are built to withstand the strength of a Troll, and considering the beating I'm still recovering from, I've got the brute strength of an infant right this moment.

Instead of planning my grand escape, I lie on the cot and feel sorry for myself. My ribs, chest, and head alternate aching and throbbing. Blood and whiskey coat my body. I rub a hand across my face and through my hair. The blood pins the hair off my forehead.

"Pssst, hey," the whisper comes from the cell across from mine. "Hey, Standard, what are you in for?"

"I'm no fucking Standard."

"What are you then?" The voice is a hiss. Too high pitched to be a Troll, too docile to be a Hair. It's missing the distinct lisp of a Sharp. I'd put money on Mage.

"I'm none of your damn business is what I am." Talking hurts. I wish this guy would shut up.

"You a Mage?"

"No."

"Hair?"

"No."

"Definitely not one of those rotten Sharps, right?"

"Right."

"You sound too small to be a Troll. So no Sharp, Mage, Hair, and too calm to be a Stone. That makes you rare."

There are plenty of other races out there, but he named the big few. He's right, my kind are fairly rare. We're part of a dying breed, ironically enough.

"What I am, is tired and beat half to death. So if you could keep quiet, that'd be peachy."

"Maybe you're a nymph."

"Fuck you."

"Selki?"

This asshole requires getting off my ass. I summon every bit of energy I have to get to my feet, cross the cell, and look out through the bars. The entire cell area is dark as a horror movie. City saves on power bills by lighting an entire hallway with one 120watt bulb.

My neighbor's cell is pitch black, and there's no sign of movement. "What do you want?"

"I wanted to know what you are, but now that you've come closer, I can see. Nice to see you, Mr. Flint." A fragile looking old man presses against the bars. White hair hangs down past his shoulders.

In all honesty, I'm too tired to be unnerved or frightened. I'm mostly just annoyed. "You know my name, neat trick."

"And what you are, Immortal."

"Quasi-Immortal."

The Mage huffs. "Aren't you all."

"And what else do you know?"

"Hmmm, wouldn't you like to know." The pale man smiles. His teeth are either chipped or missing and the gesture lights up eyes that are milky enough to make me wonder if he can even see out of them.

I throw my hands up. "I'm done. I don't need any mind games today."

"But don't you want to know about your parents?"

I freeze, my back turned to the strange old man. "What do you know about my parents?"

The old man cackles with laughter. "Do I have your attention now, Mr. Flint? That's good. You have your mother's stubbornness. Your father's blue eyes, but definitely Jane's fire."

"Tell me what you know, or shut your mouth."

My parents went missing forty years ago. The last I heard they were going to meet a prospective client down in Necrotown. Probably part of the reason the place has always given me the creeps. Paranoia makes me think my parents died down there. My heart makes me hope they didn't. One day, I will find out what really happened to them.

"Nothing is free, my boy, information least of all."

Deep breaths. I grab the bars of my cell to have something to hold. The answer of my parents' death would be great, but this old man could be lying. The past is the past, and I'm not going to go chasing down any rabbit holes over something I can't control.

"What do you want?"

The old man smiles. He runs a rough tongue over chapped and broken lips that look like they haven't seen water this year. "I want what any man wants. I want my freedom. I've been locked up too long, Sam, and I think you are just the man to free me."

"Fuck you. I'm not breaking you out of prison because you might have information."

A series of quick clacks comes from the stairwell that leads out of the cell block.

"Now if you'll excuse me, my ride is here."

The old man fades back into the shadows of his cell. "Have it your way, Samuel Flint, but when you are ready to know about what your parents, Lloyd Burgess, and Sarah Roswell have in common, you'll come back to me."

Interesting. A little part on the inside of me wants to know what he's talking about, but the bigger part doesn't care. I'm not here to suss out any family drama, mine or Burgess'. There's no telling if the guy is full of shit or not. Not worth it. Not right now, at least.

The steady 'tick-tock' of heels on concrete comes my way. The song carries the exact force and cadence of a pissed off wife. I look into the back of my cell—no shadows to fade into.

A tall, skinny guard leads Fox down to my cell. She's wearing the prettiest evening gown she owns. The sleeveless dress gives room for Sune to drape herself across Fox's shoulders, her chin on the front of one shoulder, tail on the other. The fox tattoo's lips are pulled back in mocking laughter. Fox, however, has the face of a woman about to be arrested for spousal abuse. Good thing we're already at the jail; it saves her the embarrassing ride in the back of a cop car.

"What has he done this time?" Fox turns to face the cell. Her expression softens when she sees me. "What the hell happened?"

"Public intoxication, ma'am," the guard says. His voice is tall and twangy, not a Mountain City accent, somewhere farther south, somewhere in Kentucky or Virginia, maybe.

"Public intox? Are you shitting me?" I squeeze the bars with all my post-concussion might; the iron screams in agony, or maybe that's just the head trauma.

"A concerned citizen said you were belligerently screaming and threatening him. He called us after you fell down drunk, said he was concerned for your safety." The guard slides his baton out with one hand and snatches his keys in the other.

My vision is blanketed in red. My jaw clenches. I pull against the bars just to feel the resistance. "Was this 'concerned citizen' seven feet tall and built like a skyscraper?"

The guard grunts something. "I can't disclose that. Now listen, this nice woman is here to bail you out, are you going to cooperate so I can get rid of you?"

I release the bars and step back, hands up in an 'I surrender' pose.

Guard grips his baton tighter and opens the gate. He slides the door to the side, turns, and walks away silently.

"Mr. Personality, huh?" I say.

Fox shrugs. "Come on."

I take one step. A few busted ribs and a world full of bruises remind me of the beating I received. Hunching over, I wrap my arms around my midsection.

Fox rushes in, holding me upright. "Holy shit, are you okay?"

"We seem to owe the Trolls some money; they would like that in the near future." I rest against her shoulder, using it for support.

Necrotown: Mountain City Chronicles

"Come on, let's get you out of here and to an Herbalista." Fox helps me hobble my broken ass down the hallway. "Good thing I drove."

Chapter 4

The guard has stationed himself back at his desk. Talking into a radio on the desk, he says, "There's a disturbance on the corner of Pretorious and Fifth, Officer Quig, please respond." The guard stops talking to glare at us as we make our way to the front doors.

The glass double doors swing in as no less than seven cops push past with a pair of Hairs. The two werewolves are restrained in handcuffs, ankle shackles, and muzzles—although in human form, the muzzles are a bit much. Hell, the whole thing is a bit much as both Hairs look worse than I do.

One of them, a kid in his early 20's, if I had to guess, has both eyes swollen shut and a wicked limp. The other, a slightly older male in maybe his early 30's, has a rope burn around his neck and his clothes are torn to shreds. As they get hustled past, I notice anti-shift brands on both of their necks.

The symbol is a crude drawing of a dog eating its own tail. When burned onto a Hair, they can't shift. By nature, Hairs heal faster than the normal human, so the brands will be gone in a day or two, but they are stuck in human form until then. It's normal procedure for cops to brand wolves when they arrest them, but these marks aren't fresh. A day old at least.

Fox watches with a kind of sorrow she doesn't show often. She's not some ice cold killing machine, but if I didn't know any better, I'd say she was about to scoop these pups up into her arms and take care of them. I would ask her, but if it's for me to know, she'll tell me.

"What're the charges?" The guard who let me out says.

"They got in a fight with a couple of the boys downtown," the cop in front says. He's a beefy guy with less neck than IQ points by the look of him.

"If they look like that, I'd hate to see what the Standards look like," Fox says.

Every cop in the station turns a fire-hot glare on Fox. Standards don't so much care to be called Standard. Fox stands tall in her evening gown. If these guys were half-intelligent, they'd be shitting themselves right now. Sune is still draped across Fox's shoulders, but the tattoo is foaming at the mouth from snarling.

"Charges aren't being pressed against them. These Hairs are the ones that did all the instigatin.' And got what they deserved from the looks of it."

"That's bullshit," the younger Hair yells.

No-neck cop cracks his baton across the kid's jaw. The crunch of bone echoes through the room. The kid yelps, and his legs give out. The cops on either side of him strain to hold the Hair upright.

"You son-of-a—" Fox moves forward.

I wrap my arm around her. Into her ear I whisper, "Now's not the time. Let's not fuck up Standard/Hair relations any more than they already are by killing a station full of the boys in blue to free these kids."

Fox wheels on me, blue eyes burning with rage. I already know every argument she's about to throw my way.

"Let me help. I know a good lawyer that owes me a favor. I'll give her a call, she'll take the case," I say.

"Fuck getting them out of jail, the piece of shit Standards almost killed these kids. Look at what they did." Fox's voice is anything but a whisper.

A half-dozen hands tighten around batons. Out of the corner of my eye, I catch at least one reach for his pistol. That's the smart one.

"You have to pick your battles, you know that. We can't do any good for anyone right now. Let's do this the legal way, and see about getting these kids back in their families' arms."

The younger kid watches me through swollen eyes. He's silently pleading with me to not leave him here with these animals. I want to explode. I want to help Fox murder every one of these corrupt-cop assholes. You can't always get what you want, though.

"What are these boys' names?" I ask.

"Lance Browncoat and Jebediah Thrope," no-neck asshole says.

"Their lawyer is Sandra McClain. You'll be hearing from her shortly, and I suggest not laying another fucking finger on these kids, or she will own this department."

A wave of bitching passes around the room. Sandra McClain is the best civil rights lawyer in Mountain City. She will eat these dipshits alive and do it with a smile. It won't make up for what these kids have been through, but it's a start.

"Come on," Fox wraps her arm back around me, "let's get you out of here." She puts a hand on the door and looks over her shoulder. "Boys, hang in there."

The two Hairs exhale breaths they must have been holding for hours. They sway, on the edge of collapse. Could be from relief, could be from the beating. Either way, I'll call Sandra, and she will be bleeding heart all over this thing by the next round of news cycles.

I have to lean against Fox with every step. Broken ribs grind against each other. The whole thing hurts almost as much as rebirth. Okay, not that much, but at least rebirth is over somewhat quickly and doesn't require me going to some quack Herbalista.

Out the front door of the precinct, the afternoon sun burns my eyes. This causes me to squint. This causes my forehead to wrinkle and tear open whatever scabs had stopped the flow of blood on my skull. A trickle of crimson runs down my face, and I wipe the blood off with my sleeve. This shirt is all but ruined anyway.

Once I can see again, my legs wobble with relief when I spot Fox's twenty-five year old, broke-ass sedan. Thankfully, she parked close to the entrance. Probably did it so she didn't have to walk as far in her sky-high heels, but I'm happy for the short trek either way. Fox yanks at the door handle. The door drops two inches on sagging hinges and swings open with a groan. She helps me into the passenger seat. I creak out a sound similar to the door.

Fox straightens away from the car and pushes the door closed. It catches on the running board and doesn't shut. She growls as she rips the thing open and slams it again with all the delicacy of a sledgehammer. As she gracefully stomps her way around to the driver's side, I catch a glimpse of Sune on the back of her shoulder, shaking with a silent laughter.

The driver's door has decent hinges, but the outer handle is broken. Fox leans in the open window and pops the latch. I catch an eyeful of everything her gown is no longer covering. Turning for a better view, my busted up body reminds me of exactly how little shape I'm in to be getting it on. Not that I'd let a few broken ribs stop me.

"What are you smiling about?" Fox slides in the car, cranks the key, and the car shakes, rattles, and rolls to life.

"Nothing." I turn toward my window to hide my smile.

Fox puts the sedan in gear and pulls straight into traffic without a glance. At least three different cars lay on their horns to let her know how they feel about the maneuver. She puts a silk-gloved hand out the window and gives them all a one-finger wave with the style and grace of a beauty queen.

"Can you believe that shit?" Fox uses her teeth to tug a glove off her hand. Her skin underneath is soft enough to make the silk jealous.

"Sadly, I can. This mess with the Standards and Hairs is getting bad. Things are going to erupt eventually, and I plan on staying right the hell out of it." I've been around the block long enough to see all this happen.

Call it racial tension or outright racism, either way, the Standards always have it out for someone. Too bad for the mutts, the crosshairs have been on them for quite some time now. I'll give it to the fur-balls, though, they've been having shit heaped on them since, well, since Ethan's father supposedly killed Burgess's wife.

"You're working for the head of the Hair Witch Trials," Fox says, "Do you think you can just lay low?"

She's got a point. "This job has nothing to do with the Hairs. They spend as little time in Necrotown as I do. Let them have their war. I'm going to find this kid, get paid, and we are out of here."

Fox takes her eyes off the road to stare at me. "Really?"

"Yeah. There's nothing here for us. Let's get this job done and hit the beach. I've got a nice little spot on the coast of Florida picked out."

Horns blare.

Fox turns her attention back toward the road and swerves into her lane. "Okay. Let's do it. Find this rich brat and get out of here."

I watch out the window at all the vague, gray skyscrapers reaching into the heavens. Downtown is a whole different ball game from the Glow. This place is all Standard big business. All races are accepted Downtown, but only the successful folk are welcome. This place isn't for me. Mountain City in general isn't for me. It's time to go. Time for both of us.

Fox jerks the wheel to the right and merges onto the interstate south, back towards the Glow and out of Downtown. The sharp turn tosses me against the door. I suck in a breath. Like that stands any chance of dulling the pain in my side. Yeah, right.

"You okay?" Fox rubs her hand down my cheek.

"I will be after we get this Herbalista trip over with. Have you got any money?"

"Umm, you took the check, remember?" She reaches into the back seat for a gray hoodie.

"About that. Ol' Brutus looted my pockets for payment."

Fox's palm strikes the steering wheel. The entire car shakes. Smart car. "Fuck."

"Speaking of, how did you pay the cops?"

"I had to call and borrow the money from Burgess." Fox pushes a loose lock of orange-red hair behind her ear. "Oh, yeah, you're officially on the case, by the way."

"Fuck. I need a smoke." I pat down my pockets, scan the glove compartment, scour the floorboards, and move around a pile of trash from the back seat and come up empty. "You got any cigarettes?"

Fox arches an eyebrow to the moon. "And where exactly would I keep any extras in a dress like this?"

"For cigarettes? You'd find a way."

Fox reaches into her fiery up-do and slides a pair of smokes out from inside the bun. She hands them both to me.

"See? I knew you had some hiding in there somewhere." I press in the lighter on the dash. "Speaking of, what's with the fancy getup?"

Any contentment on Fox's demeanor vanishes. The fox tattoo slinks its way off her shoulders and buries its head down the side of her ribs. "Well, now that you ask, I planned to use that big ass check you got last night for you to treat me to a special dinner, remember?"

The lighter pops. I grab it and check the end. Not hot. I punch the dash and slam the little chrome lighter back in place. It pops immediately back out. I shove the heel of my palm against it. The lighter stays this time. "So what happened?"

The fierce stare Fox turns on me could stop traffic. Not like that would matter. She has her full fury turned on me and doesn't seem to give much of a damn what's happening on the road. "That was all before someone got beat up by a Troll, robbed, and arrested. Do you know how much I had to borrow from Burgess to get you out of jail?"

Lighter clicks out again. I check again. Glowing red this time. I have enough time to light both cigarettes before it decides to die again. "How much?" I ask with a puff of smoke.

"Fourteen hundred dollars."

"Holy fucking shit." The cigarettes fall out of my mouth. "Ah, shit. Shit, shit…" I chant as I try to dig them out without any significant burn or upsetting my tender ribcage. Once in hand, I pass one to Fox and take a long draw off mine. "You should have just left me in there. No way in hell am I worth that kind of money."

"You're just lucky you're pretty." Fox winks.

"I'm not one thousand four hundred dollars worth of attractive."

Fox shrugs. "Yeah, but I think you can find our missing girl. Besides, Burgess is covering expenses. This was just an added expense."

I smile around my cigarette. "Babe, I like the way you think." Smoke gets caught in my chest. I cough. Chest muscles contract around broken bones. I yelp in between coughs.

"Aww." Fox drops her hand to my thigh and squeezes. Her grip grounds me from the flight of pain. "Don't worry, we're almost there."

The high rises of Downtown trickle off. Forty stories become twenty become ten become two become shit holes, and suddenly, we're back home in the Glow.

"Hey, babe," I say.

"Yeah?"

"Sorry I ruined dinner."

"It's okay. You can make it up to me with a road trip. I can't wait to pack." Fox giggles and tromps the accelerator. The car speeds up an astonishing seven miles per hour with a hearty puff of black smoke in the rear view.

Chapter 5

While we are on the outskirts of the Glow, it's still serene—the Standards keep extra enforcement on the borders to keep any of the grime from mucking up their business district. I pick up Fox's phone and dial Sandra McClain. I did some work on one of her cases a couple years back and got some solid information by some less-than-solid procedures. She told me she owed me big, and I just never needed to call on the favor until now.

"Well, if it isn't Sam Flint," she answers. "How have you been?"

"Not too bad," I lie. My rib feels like it's about to poke a hole in something vital. "Hey, remember that favor you owe me? I need to call it in."

Sandra laughs. Her voice is thick. She carries the same courtroom gusto even when she's out from behind the defendant's table. "That's been how many years back now? Jesus, I had just started my practice. You got me the break on my first big case."

"I didn't realize it had been so long. Sorry to call out of the blue after all this time."

"I suppose time moves different for someone who doesn't age." In the background ice cubes clank against glass.

I check the clock on the radio—seven PM. My mouth waters at the thought of a drink. So what if I still reek of whiskey? Smelling like it and tasting it are two entirely different things.

"What can I do for you, Mr. Flint?"

"I was down at the station a little earlier, and the boys in blue brought in a couple Hair youths. One was early twenties, the other early thirties, and both were beaten half to death."

The sound of the ice stops. "You have my attention."

"The cops said there was a confrontation between the Hairs and a couple Standards, but there weren't any normals getting arrested today."

"I see."

Fox nudges me. "Tell her about the rope burn."

"Oh yeah, the older one had a rope burn around his neck. His clothes were pretty ripped up, too."

"Jesus Christ." The ice resumes a steady chiming against a glass. "What do these people think this is? Birmingham in the sixties?"

"Sometimes I wonder. So would it be too much trouble for you to look into their case?"

"What are their names? I'll get right on this one."

I can almost hear the publicity wheels grinding to life in Sandra's head. "Their names are Jebediah Thrope and Lance Browncoat."

"I've got it. Thanks for thinking of me with this one. I'm always down to help out some poor, underrepresented youths. Stuff like that is great for ratings. You take care of yourself, Sam."

The phone line clicks dead, and I thank god. The conversation was just starting to make me feel slimy.

"Great for ratings?" Fox says. She probably heard Sandra's voice, god knows she talks loud enough.

"Her motives might not be pure, but she will get those guys out of lockup faster than anyone in the county. I guarantee it."

"As long as she does that, I suppose."

Fox seems genuinely worried about these kids. I'd ask her questions to find out more, but that goes against our vows. Besides, I hurt too much to give it any thought.

I shift in my seat, trying to relive some of the pain from my side. It doesn't help.

Fox squeezes my thigh again. "How are you holding up, champ?"

"Other than feeling like I've gone fifteen rounds with Tyson? Pretty good."

"Smartass."

Fox cuts off the interstate, and we hit the lower east side of the Glow in ten minutes. Downtown's muted functionality is gone, replaced by neon lights and inhabitants who are more open about their addictions than the business suit types. Decrepit street corners and well-lit storefronts display delicacies: Prostitutes wrapped in latex (or lace); dealers flashing needlepoints and misting the air with powder (sniff for a free sample); pack-less Hair arms dealers with trench coats full of pistols (buck shot, hollow points, or incendiary?); black market organs for sale (guaranteed disease free or your money back); rent-boys in rhinestone-laden leather and rock and roll.

"I hate it down here sometimes," I say, eyeing a three piece band playing on the corner.

The guitarist stands tall in his outfit consisting of leather chaps and nothing else. He's got his guitar amp hardwired into a crosswalk light. The light flickers every time he pounds another note of his shitty Skank Birds cover. The guitarist catches a glimpse of me staring, turns and flexes his bare ass-cheeks.

"Yup. Fucking hate it."

"Be nice. We live in this shit hole. And besides, the only Herbalista we can afford is down here." Without so much as a flash of her blinker or a tap of the brakes, Fox cranks the wheel to the right.

The old sedan squalls and screeches as it grinds to a halt. Fox kills the engine. The motor hisses once, clunks twice, and chatters a few times before coming to a final resting place.

Fox leans forward to read the yellow neon sign. "Santa Rosita's Herbs and Oddities. We're here." She gets out of the car and pulls a gray hoodie from the backseat on over her evening gown. It makes for an odd scene but somehow fits with the area.

Herbalitstas are miracle workers. They can make a concoction that tastes of cheesecake, makes the user feel like they just had sex, and bring them back from death's doorstep all at the same time. Those kinds of healers make the big bucks on the upper west side of Downtown. The shot callers and money makers pay good hard cash to stay healthy. Word is a personal Herbalista salary up there is second only to private security.

We get out and walk—well, Fox walks, I gingerly limp—through the front door. A bell chimes our entrance, and an overwhelming smell of dirt and peppermint makes me want to turn around and walk right the hell out. The kind of folk that operate this far south are down here for a reason—they couldn't make it uptown.

"You know, suddenly, I'm feeling much better." I turn toward the door, but Fox blocks my path.

She points deeper inside the room. A row of Santa Muerte statues line the path and that's not creepy as hell.

"How do you even know this person? I don't know this person."

"You know, I had a life before we met, honey. It's a rough world down here. A girl gets a little banged up and needs someone to patch the holes." Fox prods me in the back.

I take a few hesitant steps forward. All of the paintings of skulls look neat and interesting, but all of the actual skulls are creepier than an old lady's doll collection. "Why bother getting patched up? Why not just take a new body?" I part a set of beaded curtains and step into a room that's part kitchen, part fortune teller lair, part bedroom.

Fox runs a hand from her cheek down to her collar bone. "Because when I find a body as sexy as this one, I like to keep it new for as long as I can."

Metal pans clatter from across the room, drawing my attention to a tall, thin woman of somewhere between fifty and a thousand years old wearing a bright purple, metallic head-wrap.

"Rosita, hi. I'm Fox, do you remember me?" Fox steps forward and extends a hand.

Rosita smiles. The gesture doubles the substantial amount of wrinkles in her brown skin. "Si, senora zorra." The woman's black irises scan me over. "Y quien esta tu amigo? Esta guapo."

"Me esposo y hablas ingles, por favor. El no puede hablar espanol."

"Your husband should really learn the language if he's going to be coming this far south of the city." Rosita takes a seat at a wooden table. She sets her elbows down, and it rocks toward her. The Herbalista scowls at the table and swipes a black microwave dinner tray onto the floor. "How can I be of service anoche?"

"I seem to have run into something bigger and meaner than me." I take my shirt off revealing black and purple bruising all around my midsection. "I think a couple breaks, and a ton of bruising. And a facial laceration." I part my hair to show her the cut.

Rosita stands. Her table rocks back to its original position. She bends over to examine my chest and stomach. Her gold-ring clad fingers wrap into a fist, and she compares it to a round bruise on my side. The bruise eclipses the woman's hand. "That's a big reminder. I'm guessing you owe a Troll some money."

I sigh. "Yeah. Can you fix me?"

Rosita scoffs. "Si se puede. You're lucky to be alive. You must have very strong bones."

"I've had a couple, few lifetimes to build up bone density and scar tissue. You can say I've taken more than a few beatings over the years."

"Ohh, I have the pleasure of treating a Quasi-Immortal. It's been a very long time since I've seen one of your kind. I'm glad you mentioned it though; I'll have to adjust my formula. You Immortals are a strange bunch." Rosita raises an eyebrow, gaze locked on my flat stomach. "Physiologically speaking, that is."

"Right." Fox makes no attempt to hide her glare. Sune has moved to her back. Its front paws are draped down the fronts of Fox's shoulders and the tattoo's head is on the left side of Fox's neck, teeth bared, ears pinned back. "So how much to fix him?"

"For a lovely couple like you, three hundred." Rosita opens a cabinet. Three bottles of dried something and a mortar and pestle tumble out into her arms.

"Three hundred bucks for some oregano and juju?" I don't have that kind of money. Especially after getting jacked by Brutus.

"Can you do the juju?" Rosita's narrow gaze tells me exactly how much she thinks of my magical ability. "Didn't think so, guero." She drops the brown clay mixing bowl onto the table, and it rocks again. "Lay," she says as she adjusts her head-wrap.

I sigh and look to Fox. She nods toward the table. I sigh again, defeated. The rickety pile of wood moans under my weight, but holds steady enough. My lower legs hang off the edge.

Rosita pours a pile of dried leaves out of a clay jar into her mixing bowl. The leaves have the consistency of oregano, but smell closer to an old shoe. She goes back to her over-flowing cabinet. Glass clanks as she moves bottles, searching. She comes out with a tall vile full of pink liquid. Half the bottle gets emptied into the bowl, and the entire concoction starts smoking. That seems perfectly healthy.

The Herbalista uses her hand to waft some of the smoke to her nostrils. She takes a deep inhale, opens her mouth to taste the air. Her expression sours, and she grabs the bowl. "Here." She shoves the bowl under Fox's face. "Spit."

Fox's nose crunches up, whether from the request or the smell, I can't tell. Either way, she spits into the bowl. The mixture hisses, and Rosita takes the bowl away from Fox's face. With a poof, more smoke boils out. This new smoke is orange instead of white.

Orange like a fox. That's mighty interesti—

Rosita pours the contents of the bowl across my chest. The liquid boils over my midsection. Literally boils. Bubbles of burned skin pop up on my stomach. The bubbles swell and burst, oozing orange liquid like mini volcanoes. I scream from the pain. Heat sears my body from top to bottom. Flames burn in my mind; molten lava scorches my toes. My back arches off the table.

"Hold him." Rosita grabs my right shoulder, holds me down.

Fox circles to the other side, holds my left side down. I no longer have control over my body. My whole being is a mess of pain and contracted muscles.

The boiling liquid soothes to a low hiss. I slowly lower to a resting position, the pain subsiding. As my back touches the table, everything goes black.

Awareness slaps me like a palm to the face. I gasp and shoot up to a seated position. "What, the hell, was that about?" I ball my fists, the burning pain of the mixture still fresh on my mind.

Rosita smiles. "Painful, I know. But you are better now, guero. See?"

I look down at my body. The bruises, the boils, the orange goop that seeped from my body—it's all gone. I twist to the left. Right. Nothing hurts. I reach my arms overhead and stretch my whole body. Everything good as new.

"Three hundred dollars." Rosita holds out a weathered palm.

I get out my wallet. "Take a card?"

Rosita's shoulders slump. "Si, but you pay the ten buck fee." She digs into a drawer and comes out with a card slider for her cell phone. The phone is the newest, and nicest, thing in the entire storefront.

I swipe my card and approve the three hundred ten dollar fee. That will put my account back in the negative, but the complete lack of pain makes the whole thing almost worth it. The thought of the burn sends goosebumps racing up my arms. Almost. I'm ready to be done with this shit corner of town, but I've got one thing left before I leave.

"Hey, Rosita, what do you know about Bloodmonger and his new girl?" I pat my pockets for a cigarette, come up empty.

"The filthy pinche pendejo." Rosita crosses herself, bows to a portrait of the Virgin Mary.

"Yeah, I hear he's a real asshole, but can you tell me anything about his recent activity?"

"Just 'cause his ghetto butts up to mine doesn't mean I know about him. Why?"

I pick up my blood-stained shirt. It's as gross as the orange goo smeared across the wooden tabletop. At least I didn't get this on my vest. Shit. I left my vest on the sidewalk. Probably long gone now. Oh, well, back on point. "Some guy hired me to find his daughter. Seems to think she's been hanging around Bloodmonger."

"If she's been with him, she's infected. Your client should say a prayer and have a funeral because she's dead. Dead to her family. Dead to the world." Rosita snatches a pack of cigarettes out of a calavera-shaped ashtray. She offers us each one; we both oblige.

"Dead or not, her old man's willing to pay big bucks for his daughter. Anything you can tell me to help find her?"

Rosita stares through the haze of her smoke with narrow-eyed suspicion.

Fox takes the Herbalista's hand in her own. "Please, Rosa, we could use help to find this girl."

Rosita huffs. Smoke billows. "What is the girl's name? I will listen to the streets, see if they talk."

"Her name is Sarah Burgess," I say. "But she's going by Sarah Roswell."

"Do you still have my number?" Fox asks.

"A fox like you? I never forget. If I hear anything, I call you. Remember, tiempo es dinero."

"We hear you, Rosa. Just find what you can, please." Fox holds her arm out for me. "Come on, take me home."

"Thanks, Rosita. Here's hoping I never have to do that again. Dying is less painful than that." I put my shirt back on, dried blood and all, wrap an arm around Fox, and turn for the door.

The Herbalista grabs my arm. Her soft skin grips tight against mine. "How much do you love my zorra pequena?"

The answer comes without thought. "I would kill for her."

The old lady smiles. "Kill who?"

I smile back. "Everyone."

Rosita laughs and pats the back of my hand. "Now I see what my zorra sees in you, guero. And one last thing…"

I take my hand from hers and move toward the door. "What's that?"

"The healing salve, it has, side effects. It's best not to trust your eyes for the next few hours."

"Great. I'm going to be hallucinating." I move to the front door. "Let's go, Fox. We've got a girl to find."

Chapter 6

I reach through the driver window and unlatch the door.

"Just what do you think you're doing?" Fox clacks across the pavement to the driver's side of the car.

"Driving. I'm healed now. I can drive."

"Healed and tripping balls." Fox opens the door. She gets in before I have time to react. "I'll be chauffeuring for now."

She's got a solid point, so I don't argue. Instead, I slip into the passenger seat feeling like a new man. That concoction hurt like hell, but it worked. So far everything seems normal, too. Maybe the hallucination thing was just bullshit.

Fox twists the key, exploding the car to life. "So, where to, boss?"

"I dunno."

"You dunno? You're the detective; surely you aren't stumped on the first day." Fox moves the lever to reverse.

"The next step is to go to the shit hole at the bottom side of town and talk to Bloodmonger or whatever Necro we can get ahold of."

"So, let's go." Fox backs out of the parking lot.

A car swerves out of her way. This earns us a chorus of horns. Fox responds to the tunes with a wave.

"Yeah, only one problem. I might not exactly have my mind about me. The Necros are creepy enough without my brain playing tricks on me."

Necrotown: Mountain City Chronicles

Fox stomps the brake, stops the car dead in the middle of the road. This earns a few more screeching tires and blaring horns. "So where to then?"

I scratch at my chin, thinking. "You remember that shit blood dealer from back in the day? The guy that hired me to find his stash?"

Fox laughs from deep in her chest, something close to a heaved exhale. "Yeah, he had gotten high on something and hid it in his own refrigerator. He had to sell the whole batch for a loss because the blood smelled like pickles."

"That's the one. Doesn't he operate down here somewhere?"

"Yeah, somewhere, but I don't exactly remember where." Fox cranks the wheel and floors it.

Necros use blood for all sorts of shit, spells and rituals and whatever else. They think there's power in blood. The dipshits can't see the forest through the trees. Magic is in the air. You just have to learn how to take it. So the Necros kick back in their tent city sipping on AB negative while the real mages uptown work with little more than a thought.

Either way, they have to get their blood from somewhere, and Jimmy the blood dealer might know something about them. He owes me a favor or two, so hopefully I can cash those in for information.

Fox takes a left onto the main drag through the Glow. On the corner a man stands wearing jeans that have been ripped into shorts. He's holding a cardboard signs that reads, 'Har Sex. $10 as man, $60 as wulf.' If it's been said once, it's been said a million times, a Hair separated from its pack is a pathetic sight. The man shakes like a scared Chihuahua. Could be cold. Could be DTs. No telling.

The Hair snaps his head toward the car. His face turns to a werewolf, and he snarls at me. Claws rip though the human chest as the beast changes, prowling after me.

Wait a minute. That's not how Hairs change.

"Fox, you see this?"

"See what? The sorry fucker with the sign? Yeah, I don't think he's worth ten bucks either."

Okay, she's not freaking out. It's just a hallucination.

"Yeah, right," I say, hoping I played it off well enough.

Fox takes a right at the next corner. A building takes up half this block. Stewart's. It's a one stop shop for magical types and the nicest looking building in the Glow. All the magical lowlifes and fuck-ups get their herbs, potions, rocks, bones, and knives here. As we pass, a short black man walks out the door of the shop, brown package wrapped in twine tucked under one arm.

"Hey," I say, "isn't that Dexter?"

"I'll be damned." Fox moves the car over to the sidewalk.

Dexter Bridges. He's a small time fortune teller and big time wallet snatcher. He'll read your palm and swipe your cash, all in one friendly transaction. Word is, if it happens on the streets of the Glow, he knows about it.

I lean out my window. "Hey, Dexter, buddy."

Dexter takes one glance at me and sprints down the sidewalk.

"Goddammit." Fox accelerates to hang next to the runner.

The last time Dexter saw us we were asking for information. I asked nicely, and he didn't play along. When we got tired of asking the same question and not getting an answer, well, I may have broken three of Dexter's fingers. But that was months ago.

Dexter sprints for an entire block before slowing. Short legs and sneaky hands don't do shit for cardiovascular endurance. Fox slows the car to keep next to him.

"Hey, Dexter, come on. We've just got a question for you," I say.

"Yeah…" Dexter swallows a gulp of air. "I know… all about… your questions." Dexter stops and hunches over, hands on knees. "How many fingers you gonna break this time?"

I smile. "None, if you answer the question."

Dexter stands up, searches the street. Probably searching for backup. He leans in the window. "Fine. What do you want?"

"We just need to know where we can find that dip-shit blood dealer. Jimmy something." I pat my pocket for a cigarette. Still empty.

"Why do you want to know?"

"We need to ask him a couple questions, that's all."

Dexter huffs. "You going to break his fingers, too?"

Fox leans over so Dexter can see her. "Depends on how he answers. Besides, better his fingers than yours, right?"

"Y'all are fucking crazy." Dexter holds up his right hand. The three smallest fingers arch to the left. "I want you to know I couldn't beat off for a month without swallowing a Hydro first."

Fox snatches a small pistol from under the dash. She points it across my lap at roughly the level of Dexter's crotch. "Answer the fucking question or you ain't gonna have nothing left to be playing with."

"Fucking Christ, woman." Dexter runs his hands over his bald head, interlocks his fingers at the back of his neck. "Jimmy's been dealing over on Elmont. Stupid fuck keeps going farther and farther south. I keep telling him not to mess with those Necros, but he swears there's good money in it." Dexter shrugs. "That all?"

"Yup. Have a good night, Dexter," I say.

Dexter steps away from the car. His eyes glow red and white mist swirls around the pupils. I grip the door, trying to calm myself. Red beams creep from Dexter's eyes in my direction. I blink, trying to clear my mind. The beam gets closer. Sweat beads on my temple as the heat melts through the door. The white mist clears into white forms, people, screaming. More sweat pours down my brow as the beam gets within an inch of my face.

Fox turns the car around and takes off south toward Elmont. I exhale a breath I didn't know I'd been holding. I wipe my forehead on the back of my blood-stained, whiskey-soaked sleeve. I need a drink.

"You okay?" Fox sets her hand back on my thigh. "Seeing things?"

"No. I'm fine."

"Uh-huh," Fox says in the tone that says she knows I'm full of shit and would I please just be truthful before she has to beat it out of me.

"Okay, fine. A little, but I'll be okay."

"If Dexter back there freaked you out, I'd say it's a good thing we avoided the Necros."

"Yeah. Good thing. How far are we from Elmont?"

Fox leans forward to read a street sign over the intersection. "Not far. Few blocks. The Glow is a small place."

"Great. I can't wait to get back home and sleep this one off." I adjust my seat. The broken-ass thing has two settings, 'upright' and 'head on the back seat.' I choose the later.

Necrotown: Mountain City Chronicles

Fox reaches out and wraps her fingers in mine. She hums as she drives. I try to place the tune. The melody sounds like something out of a blues bar, but I can't name it. Three Shades of Blue, maybe. The Blue Notes? Something. Whatever the song, it sounds like a hymn on Fox's lips. A kind of down home healing as powerful as any Herbalista concoction.

My eyelids get heavy, start to droop. The world fades to a smear of noise and blurry neons. My body tingles as the gentle buzz of the off-balance tires act like a shitty hotel massaging bed.

"Hey, I think I see him," Fox says from somewhere in Asia. Japan, maybe. Wherever she is, it's a long way away.

My insides sway as the car slows.

Fox says, "Is that you, Jimmy?"

I crack open an eye. A figure hovers over me, head leaned in the car. The ghastly white ghoul's eyes glow. The ghost opens its mouth, and the sound of every the demon in Hell comes out.

I jump.

I scream.

I punch the ghost in the face.

Wait. Can you punch a ghost in the face? I don't remember being able to punch spectral beings in the face. Something about being dead excludes you from the hassle of broken noses.

"Ahh," the ghost wails. "What the fuck is wrong with you, man?"

The ghost sounds an awful lot like the blood dealer, Jimmy.

"Oh, shit." Fox opens her door and walks around to the ghost.

I move my seat upright. Outside the car, Fox is comforting Blood Dealer Jimmy.

"What the fuck, man?" Jimmy points a finger at me. His hand is bloody from holding his broken nose.

"Jimmy. Jimmy," Fox says. "Calm down. Sam's a little dopey right now."

"Dopey. Fucking right. Your boyfriend's about to be a little dead right now, bitch." Jimmy reaches for a revolver in his waistband.

The hand almost gets closed around the butt of the gun before Fox drives her right palm into the bridge of Jimmy's broken nose. Blood sprays the air as he screams and hunches over in pain. Fox slams her elbow on the back of Jimmy's neck, driving him face first into the pavement. Jimmy rolls to his back, spitting blood and profanities. Fox takes the gun out of his pants and gives him a stiletto heeled stomp to the gut as a thank you.

"Sam, you think you could grab us a room?" Fox has the gun vaguely pointed in Jimmy's direction, but he's more concerned with remembering how to breathe.

I get out of the car. We are conveniently parked in front of a motel. The place has half a dozen rooms, none of which have been cleaned this month. From where I'm standing, I can count at least three doors with lines down the middle from having been kicked in. Could be cops. Could be jealous lovers. Maybe greedy pimps. This far south in the Glow, anything goes.

"I'm going to need cash for a place like this." I nod at the cut-rate motel.

Fox reaches into Jimmy's pockets. He doesn't bother trying to stop her. All the fight drained out of him along with his blood and machismo. Fox removes three small vials of blood, two pint bags of crimson, and a small wad of cash. She flips through the bills.

"Here." She tosses me the bankroll. "That should be enough. I'd be willing to bet you can get us at least an hour in there."

I pocket the money and head for the manager's office. A sign that reads, "CH AP RAT S, NO Q STI ONS SKED," leans up against the office wall.

"Excuse me, sir, I'm in need of a room," I say through the bulletproof glass. Wonder if that glass is herpes-proof, too. Seems like that would come in handy around these parts.

The manager takes me in with an untrusting eye. He could just be squinting though. The guy has a horseshoe of shock white hair and a goatee that hangs down to his desk. "How long?" The manager grabs a can of boiled peanuts off his desk and throws one in his mouth. The ends of his goatee dip in his coffee with every chew.

I glance over my shoulder. Fox is picking Jimmy up off the pavement. "I'd say an hour will do."

The manager stands, taking a better look at Fox and Jimmy. "It'll be extra to cover the blood. Seventy-five. Cash."

I flash Jimmy's anemic roll of cash. "This cover it?"

The manager shrugs. "Close enough. Set it on the ledge."

Other than the metal speaker, the glass wall of the office is solid. No hole for money to pass. No slide out banker's drawer. I shrug, place the money on the ledge against the glass.

The manager puts his hands out. A trail of blue mist leaves his palms. The mist travels through the glass, wraps around the cash, and flows back to his palms, bringing the money with it.

Either Mr. Manager's got some magic in his back pocket, or I'm still stoned off my ass. Whatever. The answer doesn't matter.

I count pockmarks in the glass as the manager digs through stuff on his desk. A handful of nine millimeters, a couple .22s, and at least one person went big and took a pot shot with a .357—my gun of choice.

The blue mist returns and drops a key on my side of the window.

"Room six. You've got one hour, starting right now."

I take the key, meet Fox and Jimmy halfway across the parking lot. Fox is frowning at a splotch of blood on her hoodie sleeve, and Jimmy has both hands pressed against his thoroughly broken nose. I flash the key to Fox. "Room six. You were right, we've got an hour."

"Hopefully we don't need near that long." Fox prods Jimmy in the back, guiding him toward the last room in the row.

The door to room number six stands strong as a stick of hay in a tornado. This is one of the doors with a vertical crease running the center line. A hole at head level signifies where the peephole used to be.

I put the key in the handle and give it a turn. With a shove the door swings open, and a gust reeking of graveyard rot greets us. I cough, put my nose in the crook of my elbow. Fox gasps and covers her mouth with the side of her jacket. Broken nose Jimmy even flinches.

"Oh my god," Fox says, words muted through her hoodie. "What is that?"

"The motto of this place is 'No questions asked.' Let's not ask questions, and get this over with." I grab Jimmy by the shirt and drag him in the room.

A single, king bed rests against the left wall. The comforter is in the floor and a set of rumpled black sheets top the bed. The center of the fitted sheet has a dark circle the size of a dinner plate. I have no desire to find out what made the stain.

A bathroom is across from the entrance. The hinges stand lonely without a door to hold. Another victim of this shit hole. The toilet is in direct view, seat up, brown water floating at rim level. The smell of the water doesn't even make a dent in the rotten stench that hit us when we opened the door.

Fox steps in behind Jimmy, closes the door, and swings the lock-bar shut. Holes dot the frame where the lock has been ripped out and remounted multiple times. Four gashes line the back of the door. Width and length suggests they came from a Hair.

"Looks like someone took that guy up on his puppy love." Fox traces her painted-red fingernails down the claw marks.

"Or a Hair found some dinner." I grab a chair—the only other piece of furniture in the room—and sit Jimmy down. "Hi Jimmy. I feel like we got off on the wrong foot back there."

Jimmy snarls, showing off blood-smeared teeth. "You broke my fucking nose."

"That was an accident," I say.

Fox coughs. "Sam was an accident. I punched you on purpose." She pulls her dress away from her body and examines the hem. Black marks mar the beautiful fabric. They must be from grime in the parking lot.

"And you fucked up my dress." Fox indicates the smear of blood on her hoodie. "And my favorite sweatshirt. I should break more bones just for that."

Jimmy shivers, but pushes himself up straight in his chair. He juts his chin out like the tough guy he's not. "So, what do you want?"

Fox holds out one of Jimmy's pint bags. "Still dealing blood I see. O neg even. That's the fancy shit."

"Yeah, no laws against dealin' a little of the red stuff. Not this far south." Jimmy eyes the bag like liquid gold.

For him it pretty much is. A pint of O neg is worth some bucks. He doesn't even have to deal strictly to the Necros either; Sharps pay good money for blood. They use it to cook flesh, some kind of seasoning or something. Sharps are weird—weird and vicious.

"That's fine." I set a hand on Jimmy's shoulder.

Jimmy flinches.

"We're glad you're still selling. We need to ask you some questions about your buyers." I tighten my grip.

"No way, man. No fucking way. Dealer-buyer confidentiality, bro."

I squeeze tighter. Something in Jimmy's shoulder pops. "Let's not do this the hard way, Jimmy. We aren't asking you for names and addresses."

"Well, not yet, anyway." Fox licks her palm and rubs at the dark spot on her jacket. Sune is on the back of Fox's hand, sniffing at the stain.

Jimmy's gaze darts between Fox and me. "Fuck you guys. I'm not saying anything."

"You don't even know our question," I say.

"Don't matter much. I've only been dealing to one group lately, and if you're asking about them, then I'm more scared of them. You and the sexy redhead over there ain't got shit on them, bro."

I lean my head back, stare at the ceiling. Dark spots are spattered across the popcorn in an arc. I take a deep breath, summoning patience. "Okay, so you've been dealing solely with the Necros, right?"

Jimmy shakes. Stays silent.

"Why are you afraid of them?" I say. "Sure, they're creepy, but harmless. They can't hurt you like we can."

"Th-tha-that was then, bro. This is now. Things are different."

"Ah, progress." Fox gives up on her dress and drops it. The hem of the satin brushes across the stained shag of the carpet.

"Have you been dealing to Bloodmonger?" I step back and face Jimmy. Better position to judge his answers.

Jimmy stares at the carpet.

"Oh-kay. I'll take that as a yes. Do you know anything about a new girl? Sarah Roswell."

Jimmy doesn't lift his gaze, but he shakes at the mention of Sarah. His wooden chair creaks.

"Looks like we've hit a sore spot," Fox says. "What can you tell us about Sarah?"

Jimmy tilts his head up, smiles at Fox with a burst of cockiness. "Nothing. Sarah's dead. Gone. I don't know why you are looking for her, but I'd back off before you get hurt."

Fox rushes forward, wraps a hand around Jimmy's neck. Her tattoo moves to her forearm, snapping at Jimmy. "I don't take kindly to threats, James. Do you know what I am? What I can do?"

Jimmy glances at Sune, still snapping.

"I'll take that as a yes. Now if you don't quit showboating, my fox here is going to hitch a ride in your body." The animal moves down the tips of Fox's fingers, its snout moves to Jimmy's neck. "And we'll take a ride to Necrotown. Wonder how long I can spend in your body before I get you killed?"

Cotton rips from behind me. I look away from Fox and Jimmy. Something in the bed moves under the sheets. With another tear, a figure stands up from inside the mattress. The stained black sheet hangs over a body like a muddy ghost.

I can't help but smile. These fucking hallucinations won't get the best of me. I move toward the figure, grab the end of the sheet and pull. The person underneath used to be a man, maybe thirty. Claws have ripped away the skin exposing bone on the right side of his face. His right eye is missing. The marks continue across his chest, exposing all sorts of muscles and organs. Brown and green liquid ooze from his stomach.

The stench from earlier comes back, ten times as strong.

Yeah, subconscious, I see it. Good trick. That's creepy as hell. Neato.

Deadman tilts his shredded skull to the side, examining me with its remaining blue eye. I mimic the movement. Deadman snarls. I snarl back.

"What the fuck," Jimmy yells.

Fox screams.

Deadman grabs me by the neck, drives me into a wall.

At this point, the situation becomes extremely clear. This is not a drill. Repeat, not a drill. An actual corpse is attacking me.

I punch Deadman with a right. The corpse is pressed too close for the punch to carry any power. The attacker shrieks. Its breath smells of death and bacon.

A wooden chair crashes across the corpse's back. Fox stands behind it, chest heaving, broken slats of wood in her hands.

I reach for the gun on my belt. My fingers wrap around the butt. I get the gun clear and fire two shots into the corpse. Somewhat predictably, the bullets do nothing. Deadmen fear no pain.

Necrotown: Mountain City Chronicles

The corpse wraps both hands in my shirt. It pulls me forward and drives its forehead into mine. The world goes fuzzy as Deadman drops me to the floor.

Fox swings one of the chair slats into the side of the corpse's neck. Deadman pushes Fox with one arm. She trips over the foot of the bed and lands in the hole in the mattress.

The corpse advances toward Jimmy.

"No, no, please," Jimmy begs. "I didn't tell 'em nothin'. You got to believe me." Jimmy puts his hands out in front of him.

Deadman grabs the sides of Jimmy's face.

"No. Please. No—"

A twist of the hands snaps vertebrae. He drops dead Jimmy to the floor.

I fire two more shots at the body. Both bullets connect. Neither do anything more than annoy the corpse.

Deadman stomps across the room. I try to scramble away, but the corpse drops a knee on my chest, holding me in place. Using my shoulders, I try to walk myself out of danger, but Deadman presses harder.

I dive into the depths of my memory, trying to wrench magic from my body, from the corpse's body, from any-fucking-where. Parrafina, a kill spell, comes to mind, but it never works for me.

Retreating further within, I summon any dormant magical prowess. A slight tug of power tingles in my core, but not enough. I extend my mind. The corpse burns with magic. Can I siphon some of it for the spell? Stealing magic feels like putting on someone else's well-used underwear. I don't even want to think about what this corpse's magic feels like.

"Fuck it." I draw on the corpse's power. When I have more than enough, I grab Deadman's chest.

Deadman's magic tastes like blood and bile and tingles the back of my tongue like making out with an electric eel. I push the image from my mind, mumble the incantation, and focus the energy outward. A black wave blasts from my hands, hits the corpse in the chest.

The corpse grabs me by the throat and leans in close, laughing. Not enough juice.

Fox emerges from the bed tangled in her satin dress, cotton sheets, and stale blood. She stands over the top of the corpse and drives the wooden slat into Deadman's back. The body doesn't flinch.

Dead Jimmy rushes out of nowhere and tackles Fox. She lands on her back next to me and Deadman. Dead Jimmy puts his knee on Fox's chest and a hand on her throat, mirroring Deadman's hold on me.

I struggle to get out from under him, but it's no use. Fox, however, is better at this hand-to-hand garbage. She sweeps Dead Jimmy off the top of her in one quick motion, picks up the chair slat, and drives it into his throat repeatedly. Between the stab wounds and the already broken neck, it doesn't take much for Fox to separate Dead Jimmy from his head. This ends the fight.

Fox is on her feet and moving toward me in a flash. Damn, that woman is quick. She swings her zombie-killer chair-slat back like a baseball bat and charges Deadman.

But as fast as she is, Deadman is faster. Before she completes her bashed-skull-home-run, Deadman grabs me by the ears and snaps my neck with entirely too little effort.

Dying hurts.

Dying and leaving your wife in a room with a zombie is a massive exercise in patience. The process takes as long as it takes, and the pain is somewhere north of a healing salve from Herbalista Rosita. Rebirth is the world's worst agony. I can be called a phoenix of sorts. I die, just like anyone else, but I don't stay dead.

In three minutes my corpse disappears. Vanishes. Puff, gone like a ninja. After that is a period that lasts anywhere from ten minutes to an hour—during this time I don't exist. Mind, body, soul—whatever, they're gone. Not one spec of Samuel Flint exists in this phase. Once whatever random amount of time passes, I begin piecing myself back together.

My mind is first. The feeling is like waking up. Well, more like being woken up by an ice bath. The return to consciousness is as abrupt as it is painful. One moment Deadman is breaking my neck like a toothpick, the next I'm an idea, floating through time and space. The whole thing is trippy as hell. The pain at this point is negligible. I don't yet have a body to hurt, just a mind to be slapped around.

Wherever I die has no effect on the next part of the cycle. I could die in central Mountain City, New York City, or outer space, and things would happen the same. Every Quasi-immortal like me has a home, a lair. This isn't a home they choose, it's where they were born. Where I came into this world is where I will come back to this world. It's not my apartment. My home is a place I return to so I can finish the rebirth. The location is secret. Fox is one of two people I've ever told. I can trust Fox; the other is dead.

My soul travels from the place I die to the lair. The journey is fast, but cold. The air chills to the core. My essence travels to my birthplace and through a chimney to the living room. This is where I was born. This is where I am reborn.

With my spirit in the proper place, it's time for the real hurt to commence. My soul contracts into a brain-sized ball of energy. From the air, my mind pulls magic from the house. The house groans, and the magical draw sucks the entire structure in toward me. The roof of the derelict house bows.

Energy in my home tastes like dust. It grates like sandpaper against my mind. Floorboards pop and warp. My body forms first as a series of nerves. The magic seeps into my consciousness and rebuilds without instruction. My nervous system floats over the floor of the house. Synapses push further and further across my body. Each one sears like an electric shock.

I would curl into the fetal position if I had any say over my body. I don't. The magic does. When the last nerve completes, the energy starts at my toes, works its way up, building bone and ligament. The bones intertwine around the nerves. The assault is excruciating.

My skull completes the bones. I flex my hands, control coming back. The power makes another pass, grafting muscle to bones and nerves. Neck muscles regenerate, creating vocal cords. I scream. My body has gone from electrocution to the inferno. The muscles burn as they weave together. My hands shake. I try to hold still. The process takes longer when I move. I've had plenty of practice, and I need to hurry up and get back to Fox.

I don't know what I'll do if anything happened to her because I died.

The last pass from bottom to top wraps my body in skin and hair. Having skin stretched taut to fit the body burns like being drawn and quartered; I know from experience. Every new hair that sprouts stings like a hair being plucked. That doesn't sound bad, but multiply it by five million. See how you feel after that.

The magic completes its job and dissipates, dropping my newly reborn, naked body on the warped floorboards of my childhood home. This is my trick, my magic. The biggest trick of all? There's no telling how many lives I have. That's why I'm a Quasi-Immortal.

I die.

I'm reborn.

One day, I will die and won't come back. Quasi-Immortals have a limit to how many times they can die. There haven't been enough studies done to figure out how it works. I have heard of Quasis permanently dying after only three rebirths, and others have been rumored to die hundreds of times before meeting a final resting place. Me? I'm somewhere in the middle of that spectrum at the moment.

I gasp. Cool air chills newborn lungs. I cough, punch the floorboard of the house. "Fuck," I yell at the top of my lungs, trying to expel the adrenaline. My body convulses. Convulsions slow to shivers. I roll to sitting, tuck knees to chest.

In an ages-old rocking chair, in her gore-stained hoodie and evening gown, sits Fox, watching me. There's a half-smile tucked at the corners of her lips. "That's the first time I've actually *seen* it, you know?"

"Yup," I say, suddenly conscious of being in a seated, fetal position. Naked in front of my wife should not feel this awkward. I try to stretch out, but my new skin is taut as fresh leather. At least I manage to stretch out slightly before the pain is too much. "I'm full of all kinds of tricks."

"Really?" Fox arches an eyebrow.

"Okay, not really. That was pretty much it right there. The Sam Flint pièce de résistance." I spread my arms out. "Tada."

Fox stand up from her seat. Her dress hangs limp, weighed down by blood and god knows what else. Stilettos clack against the wood floor of the house. She leans and kisses me on the forehead. I can't see the red lip print on my head, but I can feel it.

"Well," she says, "I think it's quite a show. I especially like the happy ending." She nods at my nakedness.

I wink at her. "A happy ending would be great, but one of us looks and smells terrible."

She kicks me in the chest, hard. I can't see the lip print, but I can sure as fuck make out the pencil-sized heel print on my sternum. Those things hurt.

"We can't all get reborn nice and pretty after a fight." Fox holds her arms out to the side and looks at her clothing. She peels her hoodie off like it's contaminated. It very well could be.

I stand up and lean into her, giving her a hug, kissing her in the same place she got me on the forehead. "I think you're ravishing. Nothing better than that just-rolled-across-a-butcher-shop-floor look." The muck and death on her dress squishes against my skin. I would move away, but the embrace is too nice. Besides, this is what showers are for.

Fox breaks the contact. "Get some clothes on, and let's get home. We need to figure out what just happened."

I keep a few changes of clothes in a dresser in the corner, ready for a rebirth. I grab a black t-shirt and use it to wipe myself off. There isn't much for a laundry hamper here so I drop the dirty shirt on the floor. That will probably stink later, but I'm not too worried about it. I grab another black shirt, jeans, steel-toe boots, and a leather jacket.

Fox is still staring at me in semi-amazement when I get finished dressing. "You know, Fox, you always see me naked. Surely you aren't still *that* impressed by this form."

"No, not at all." Fox cringes like she just killed a puppy. "Well, no, you know. Rebirth. I've never seen anything like that. It looked..."

"Painful?"

"Yeah, painful, but it was beautiful, too. Do you think many people have ever, actually seen that before?"

I bend over to lace my boots; my body protests that much movement, but I manage. "Probably not many. The only thing more secretive than a Quasi are you foxes."

Fox smiles. Sune is curled up on Fox's bicep, and the tattoo lifts a head to shake with laughter. That thing is a sneaky shit, I'm telling you. "I think you know plenty about how we foxes work." She tries to give me a coy look, but can't quite pull it off. I might not be privy to all of her past, but I know enough to understand her idea of coquettish involves razor-sharp steel and vengeance.

Truth is, I probably have as much knowledge about the Kitsune—that my wife is one sums up the total of my knowledge— as Fox knows about Quasis, but there's still a world to learn. We are both part of two of the oldest races known. With age comes secrecy. Something our ancestors were well acquainted with.

"Come on, let's go." I take Fox by the hand and lead her to the door.

"I'm not approving you dying or anything, but I could watch your naked ass get reborn all day long."

I close the door and lock it behind me. Every pair of pants has a spare key. Although it's not likely anyone can find this place, let alone try to break into it. This little cabin in the middle of nowhere looks like it was built in the middle ages; it could be an English peasant's modest home. Instead, it's my little cabin in the woods.

The driver's seat of Fox's car is covered in blood. "Uck," I say. "Why don't you drive us home? And pretty much everywhere else until we can get that seat bleached."

"Don't be such a pussy." Fox takes the driver seat. The wet seat squishes even under her slight weight.

I groan and get in the passenger seat. "What happened back there? How did you get out?"

Fox focuses on something in the distance as she drives. She doesn't speak for a minute. "I tried to save you, but I couldn't. A few seconds too late. If I were just a little faster, I could have saved one of your lives."

It's my turn to put a reassuring hand on her thigh. "It's fine, babe. I've got plenty more where that came from."

She turns a laser-glare on me. The lie was weak, and she knows it all too well. "Don't screw around, Sam. One of these days you won't come back, and I can't live without you."

"It's okay." I lean over and kiss her bare shoulder. Sune skitters across Fox's back to get away from my lips. "I'm not going anywhere."

Fox's shoulders loosen. She focuses back on the dirt road, taking it at rally-cross speeds.

"So, you killed Deadman with that piece of wood?"

"The swing connected a fraction too late. At first..." Fox swallows. "At first I thought the crack I heard was the wood against Deadman's head. But it wasn't. It was—"

"I know what it was." The snapping of my neck still rings in my ears. "What happened next?"

"I bashed that fucker's head in until there wasn't nothing left." She takes her hand off the wheel and examines the dried blood there. Her hands are almost solid crimson that turns into smears by her elbows and splatters up near her shoulders. A splash of blood is speckled across her pale cheek.

"Then you came here?" I squeeze her leg, an invitation to keep going.

"I hauled ass to try and get up here in time for your rebirth. I wanted...I wanted to see it happen, you know?"

"I know."

"I almost didn't make it. Why did you have to be born so far out here?"

"My parents thought it would be safer. They scouted this place out when mom was pregnant."

Fox nods. "That was smart of them."

Memory makes me smile. "You know what's funny?"

"What's that?"

"My mom went into labor all the way up in Hair Alley. My dad had to do something like a hundred twenty miles an hour to get her here in time."

"Holy shit. He drove faster than I do."

Hair Alley is at the northeast of Mountain City, more or less as far from my birthplace as you can get while staying in the same county.

"What were your parents doing in Hair Alley?"

"Huh. You know, I never asked. My dad liked to tell stories after a couple beers, but for as many times as I've heard that one, he never mentioned why they were up that way."

"They were probably buying a gun to keep you in line." Fox smirks. "Even in the womb they could probably tell you were going to be a problem child."

"I resent that comment." I slap the top of Fox's thigh.

After a few minutes of silence, I say, "Back at the hotel, that was a person possessing corpses, right?"

"I think so."

We've reached the outskirts of the city. Passing cars shine light on Fox, and I can see wrinkles of concern at the corner of her mouth.

"That's a lot more magic than Necros are capable of. If the lot of them pooled their energy, they couldn't animate one corpse, let alone two simultaneously."

Fox sits up straighter, pushes a loose strand of hair. "You think this is why everyone is interested in Sarah? She's the only thing new. If she has that kind of power…"

"I've never seen anything like that… from anyone. Not the high Mages Uptown, nothing. I still want to talk to Bloodmonger. He's head of Necrotown. If this…whatever, is coming from his shithole corner of the town, he will know. Nothing happens in Deadman's land without Monger knowing about it. That's my plan."

"Sounds good," Fox says. "But first I need a shower."

Chapter 7

The rest of the drive back to the apartment is covered in blood and silence. On the bright side, none of the gore belongs to Fox. On the other hand, Fox is covered in other people's blood. Probably not the romantic evening she planned.

I slide my hand from her thigh and hold her hand. She's steady as a rock, but that's no surprise. She's seen a lot in her years. A slightly raised pulse thumping against her palm is the only sign of her being on edge.

Our apartment/office has six parking spaces out front. Six slots to cover eight offices. Generally, we have to park at a garage two blocks up, but today we luck out. One space, directly in front of the door, sits open—yellow lines spread wide, an open embrace for a broke ass car.

Fox parks. I hurry around and open the door for her. Chivalry is as dead as people let it be. Not me. I've been around. Old school. Remember? I wrap an arm around her, and we head for the apartment.

The inside of our place is as I left it. Well, almost. There are four different dresses crumpled up on and around the bed. Probably Fox trying to find the perfect outfit for that dinner we never had. I add a mental memo to make that right when we get paid.

Fox slides out of her ripped and blood-stained gown, dropping the dress to the floor. Luckily, her perfect skin is unscathed, picture perfect as always. A coat of dried blood covers her milky white body. A bloody hand print across her throat jumpstarts my heart again.

Sune is curled up in a ball on Fox's lower hip, pretty much the only spot not smeared in gore. Fox steps close, grips the bottom of my shirt, and yanks it off. "You, husband, need a shower."

"I'm freshly reborn, clean as an infant." I unbutton my jeans. "But you, wife..."

"Ugh. Don't remind me. I'm trying to be all Zen and not think about it." Fox closes her eyes. She gulps like she's swallowing bile. In all fairness, she does look like the lone survivor of Carrie's failed prom.

I step out of my jeans. "Flip a coin for who gets the shower first?" With any luck she'll suggest we shower together. I am perfectly clean except for the taste of the Deadman's magic stuck in the back of my throat.

Fox guides me to the bathroom, turns on the faucet. She steps in the shower and gives me a playful wink. "It's big enough for the both of us, you know."

Hell, yes. I jump in with her for what should be the least sexy joint shower of all time. Clumps of dried gore fall off of her as soon as the water hits. Red droplets splash against the clear shower curtain and fade to pink as they runs down the side of the tub. The water at the drain pools red. Then brown. After forty minutes, and a bottle of body wash, it turns clear.

We towel off and examine each other for injuries. Okay, that shouldn't have been sexy, but running my hands over Fox's curves, searching for cuts, gets me lost in the scent of her skin. Kneeling in front of her, I slide my hands down to her hips and kiss the lines of muscles on her stomach.

She half-moans, half-laughs, and pushes me away. "You know, having a newborn nibble on my navel should be much weirder than this."

"New RE-born. I'm no baby, darling." I lean forward and kiss her again.

Fox leans back against our bathroom counter and pushes me away with her foot. Two dozen bottles of beauty products rattle as her weight rocks the vanity. A vial of perfume rolls into the sink.

She picks up a hairbrush off the sink and brushes her hair, foot still keeping me at leg's length. Her expression grows serious. "Do you want to quit? Just forget we ever heard of Sarah Roswell and Lloyd Burgess."

"Fuck no."

She tilts her head to the side, part from confusion—I think—and part to brush the other side of her hair. "Really?"

"Hell yeah, really. Rent is three months behind, and apparently I owe the Trolls some money. We'll figure out what's going on, but I'm doubling my fee. Burgess can afford it." I take a deep breath, I don't want to say this next part, but there's no point in leaving it out. "Besides, he still might be able to help with my parents. Maybe not, but if there's a chance…I have to know."

Fox runs the back of her knuckles across my cheek, a sad look on her face. "Fine, but you aren't going out without me. Trolls or zombies or whatever is out there, you could use the backup."

I open my mouth to protest.

Fox smacks me in the forehead with the back of her hairbrush. "Shut up. I'm coming."

Whatever. Fox can handle herself. I hate her being in danger, but it's not like she'll listen to me anyway. Might as well have her next to me as opposed to watching from the shadows.

With the danger momentarily over, and the gore washed away, my adrenaline dumps. All will to be conscious evaporates in a split second, and every part of my body aches. The pain and adrenaline all came from the rebirth, but it feels much the same as getting in a huge fight with a couple of corpses in a hotel room.

"You look like shit." Fox stands up, takes my hand, and leads me toward the bedroom.

"Thanks." I collapse on the bed. Fox lies next to me, cuddles up against my shoulder. Her body burns hot against mine, even through her robe.

"I'm beat." She sets a palm against my heart.

"You're telling me. I've only had two cigarettes today. And no alcohol. That fucking Troll broke my whiskey bottles."

She huffs a laugh. "After we get some answers and operating money from Burgess tomorrow, we'll stock back up on supplies."

I grunt over the thought of spilt malt.

"Hey." Fox pushes against my chest to sit up and look me in the eye. "Was that magic I saw you use earlier?"

Her question reminds me of the siphoned Deadman's magic. Bile in the back of my throat burns like acid and something slithers under my skin. Goosebumps prickle my arms. "Yeah, something like that."

"You must have been worried. I haven't seen you break out any power in years—didn't know if you still had any left in you."

"Well, there was a reanimated corpse trying to kill me." Magic is something I will never forget how to use, even if I do suck at it.

Non-Mages can learn to control magic, but it takes time. A very long time. Most people just don't have the time. I spent years training to get half-shitty at the craft. The power in the air will never be my go-to weapon, but in a tight spot I'll take what I can get.

Fox traces her fingers down my arm and around the lines in my palm. She follows them to a series of vertical scars on my forearm. For anyone else they'd be called hesitation marks, but I've never been one for hesitation. Fox slaps my chest. "Get some sleep so we can get some work done tomorrow."

I roll toward her and kiss her bare shoulder. Her skin calls to me stronger than any Siren's lullaby, singing a song of soul-deep desire. This woman has buried herself so deep in my soul that she is the only thing I care about—the only thing I've cared about in forever. I plant my lips against her collar bone. "I was thinking about something other than sleep." I kiss my way to her breasts.

A growl rolls from her chest as I shift myself on top of her. She presses her hips against mine. It's the first of many moans tonight.

Morning comes. Morning goes. Afternoon comes. Afternoon is fading quickly when I drag my ass out of bed. Fox smiles in her sleep and moans as I slide out from under her and off the bed. I start my morning brew, open a cabinet, slam it closed when there's no liquor in it. My hands shake against the counter. I need a fix. Time doesn't cure addiction; if anything, it enhances it.

I grab the phone off the nightstand and dial Burgess.

"Hello," he answers, voice cruel, expectant.

"Yes, Mr. Burgess, this is Sam Flint—"

"Do you have information on my daughter's whereabouts?" Burgess interrupts.

"Maybe, but we've run into a bit of snag and, daily expenses have proved to be a problem. I need you to front me some more money so I can continue my investigation."

Pause for a beat. Make it two.

"Very well. How much do you require?"

My turn to pause for a beat. "Two grand will cover it."

Fox wraps her arms around me from behind, nuzzles against my shoulder. Her hands trace my stomach, and I force myself to swallow a moan. That would not be something I'd want to do on a business call, but I don't move her hands either.

"I'll have three wired into your checking account, but one thing, Mr. Flint?"

"What's that?"

"Come to me for more money without concrete evidence of my daughter and they will never find the pieces of that pretty little number you carry on your arm."

The line clicks dead.

"Fuck." I slam my phone on the counter. Probably doubled the size of the cracks on the screen but what's it matter?

"What'd Burgess say?" Fox's warm body pressed against my back wakes me up and threatens to take me back to bed all at the same time. Her hands draw me to bed for a very different reason.

"Yeah. He's going… to give us more..." I can't think about anything, but Fox's hands.

"Good."

I turn around, into her, our chests touching, and kiss the top of her head.

Sunlight shines through the window and directly into my face. Dammit, what time is it? The sun is already on its way down to be shining through our windows.

I check my phone. Creeping up on three P.M. "We need to get going. Today's almost gone."

"No," Fox whispers in my ear. Her hands roam up my back, fingernails dig into my shoulders as she pulls me against her. "After a day like yesterday, you owe me at least six different kinds of massages. A girl has needs, you know."

"I know all about your needs." I smile. "Now go get dressed, you're distracting me."

Fox pouts.

I do my best to steal my jaw with resolve. It's a brave effort on my part. We've got to get to the bank before it closes or we'll be stuck for another day with no money. I need alcohol and nicotine.

And Fox. God, I need her.

Fox saunters over to the dresser and pulls out a torn up pair of jeans and t-shirt. Sune takes up residence on the inside of her left forearm. Definitely a change in scenery from her outfit last night, but probably more work friendly. Fist fights in six inch heels and silk gowns are equally as impractical as they are sexy.

"You know, there's an ATM that's open twenty-four hours a day?" she says.

"No, someone ripped the front off of it last week, remember?" I grab a shirt off the top of the dresser, smell it, deem it clean enough. I put on a clean pair of jeans and lace up my steel-toe work boots while Fox slips into a pair of orange and white Chuck Taylor sneakers.

"That's right. Buncha rednecks hooked it up to a truck and tried to drag it away, right?"

"Yup. So we have to get our money the old fashioned way—going in and talking to someone."

Fox and I both shudder.

Wallet in pocket, keys in hand, I give the room one last survey to make sure I haven't forgotten anything. "Ready to go?"

"Hell, no. You see this?" Fox points to a faint, yellow bruise on her cheek. "I can't go out like this." She disappears into the bathroom to cover the bruise, and her eyelids, and her cheeks, and her lips, and whatever else women cover in the bathroom.

She emerges a few minutes later, war paint over the bruise and everything else from her chin up. "Ready now." She hooks her arm through mine and leads me out the door.

We drive to the bank, and I run inside. Luckily, I catch a nice teller who gives me my two grand without question. After my last incident, I figure it might not be a good idea to take every penny out of the bank, so I'll leave some in case of emergency. What are the chances it's still in there tomorrow? Yeah, pretty slim, I know.

Back in the car, I fan the money out in front of Fox. Her blue eyes glow green with the reflection from the cash. She snatches the money out of my hand. "Come on, let's grab some whiskey and get wasted."

I have no arguments for this logic.

A few minutes later we park in front of Espozino's. The Gargoyle kid is still frozen rock-hard out front. Warsaw is struggling to move the statue further down the sidewalk, away from his shop.

He stops when he sees us coming. Bending at the waist, he props himself up with hands on his knees, panting. "Well, if it isn't Dorian Gray and his mistress," he spouts off between breaths.

"Fuck you, Warsaw." Fox smiles at him, letting him know she meant it in the kindest of ways.

We move past him and into his glass menagerie. Only, it's the good kind of glass menagerie, not a crappy one full of little animals. No, this place is a couple's retreat—without the annoying other couples. Doubly so since there aren't any animated Gargoyles bro-ing up the place today. Nope, just the couple random addicts, all more concerned with bottled redemption than anything else.

"Is that any way to treat your favorite barkeep?" Warsaw follows us in, brushing concrete dust or powdered Gargoyle or whatever off the front of his vest.

"Save it, Warsaw," I say. "You're not a bartender, you're a cashier."

"I ain't just a fracking cashier. I'm the owner of this here shite establishment."

I plant my palms on the counter, grin at him. "Well, as the owner and the cashier, you should be doubly motivated to sell us some booze."

Warsaw whistles. "Christ, back for more already. I just sold youse two bottles yesterday."

"I kind of dropped those and could use another pair. Same thing if you don't mind. It smelled quite nice." I reach into my pocket for the cash. Empty. That's right, Fox swiped my cash. Guess she's paying.

Warsaw sets two bottles of Kerrigan's Irish Whiskey on the counter. "Will you be having the seltzer water again as well?"

"Save the water." I tuck the bottles under my arm. "I'll be enjoying these straight."

Warsaw shrugs. "Have it your way, but be careful, it bites."

"I'll remember that. Fox, pay the man." I leave her with the bill and walk out the front door, directly into trouble.

A seven foot tall Troll stands with gray/green arms crossed over his chest. The Troll snarls to show off all three of his teeth, jagged things the size of credit cards. "Aren't you predictable," the troll says.

I'm impressed Brutus can define the word predictable. "Wait just one minute." I set the bottles of whiskey on the ground, away from the ass beating I'm about to receive.

"Money," Brutus grunts. Back to words with small syllable counts that seems more accurate.

"How much more could I owe you after everything you took last time?"

The Troll squeezes his hands into fists, knuckles cracking like tree branches. "You owe more. Interest."

"Fuck, you greedy-ass Trolls. I'm working a job, and I'll pay you when I'm damn well ready to pay you. You wanna kill me—go for it." I spread my arms wide and invite the enforcer to try his hand again.

Brutus steps forward and the concrete shakes beneath his size seventy-two boots. I take a deep breath and stagger my feet in a fighting stance. This time I'm going to punch this bastard at least once. That's my goal. He can kill me as long as I break his crooked nose first.

Fox's legs wrap around Brutus from behind. She grabs his head and yanks it back, holding a razor to his throat. I have no idea where Fox makes blades appear from, never asked, but she always has something sharp close at hand.

"Listen here, you thick-skulled fuck." Fox's voice is pure menace. "We have paid you enough. Back off, or I will cut out your tongue."

Brutus laughs. "That's all? Brutus needs no tongue."

"I'll cut it out through your goddamn throat." In a flash, Fox slices the Troll underneath one eye and jumps off his back.

"You bitch!" Brutus has both hands pressed up against his face to stem the bleeding. It's not helping much.

"Get lost or the next cut will be your last." Fox flips the blade closed and with a flourish of her hand it disappears into her...well, I don't know where it goes, it's just gone.

We all have our own sorts of magic, I guess.

Brutus stumbles away. Probably pissed and surely embarrassed, but dealt with for the moment.

One more time Fox has saved me. I'm really going to have to save her one of these days, just to balance out the scales.

I wrap an arm around my beautiful bride. "You know he's coming back, right?"

"Yup, and I'll cut his damn head off next time."

I shrug and bend to grab the whiskey. "I'll drink to that."

Chapter 8

There's one window in the entire apartment. It leads to our balcony. Balcony is an overstatement. It leads to a section of roof that is sloped gently enough to sit on without falling into an impromptu meeting with the pavement. Immortal or not, dying hurts like hell.

I climb out first and kick a couple loose shingles down.

"What the fuck!?" someone yells from below. The voice doesn't seem to be coming to kick my ass, the shingle must have missed him. I'll try harder next time.

Fox crawls out and takes a seat next to me. The half-rotten plywood that makes up the roof sags under our weight. Someone more concerned with their own mortality would probably move. We don't. Fox opens the cap on our whiskey.

She takes a healthy swig and passes the bottle. "That was Sarah the other night, right?"

"I'm not convinced. Maybe. If it was, maybe she acted under duress."

"Ohhh, a damsel in distress?" Fox bats her eyes at me and tries her best at a helpless pose, back of her hand pressed to her forehead. Helpless suits Fox about as well as spaghetti noodles are suited for supporting the Golden Gate Bridge. Sune rolls her eyes and travels up Fox's forearm, disappearing into the sleeve of her shirt.

"I dunno. What I do know is that nothing goes through Necrotown without Bloodmonger's seal of approval. He's involved with this or at least knows about it." I chug some swill and pat my pockets for a cigarette. "I'd at least like to have some words with the punk."

Fox grabs the bottle. "That means a trip actually into Necrotown." She eyes me as she slowly tips the bottle.

"And?"

The laugh that spews from Fox's throat carries two fingers of whiskey with it.

"Gross. Is that, scotch?" A woman retches below us.

"It's whiskey, you dumb broad." Fox holds the bottle over the edge of the roof as proof.

"What's so funny?" I ask.

"You're terrified of Necrotown."

"Am not."

Fox arches an eyebrow. Obviously, her bullshit detector is spiking.

"Not terrified." It comes out a pout. "I just hate it there."

"For someone who can't die, you sure are awful afraid of death."

"One: I can die. Two: I'm not afraid of death or Necrotown. That place just gives me the creeps. The Glow is a shit hole, but at least the people are obsessed with chemically or magically improving their life. Down there, in Necro, they're obsessed with death. It's just weird."

"Well, good thing I'll be there to protect my big strong man from the monsters in their coffins."

"Funny." I grab the bottle and take a drink.

Fox leans back on her elbows, looks up at the sky. "The amount of magic, to control the dead. . . it's amazing. Isn't it?"

"That's one word for it. More juice than I've ever seen for sure."

"What would you do?" Fox lays her head in my lap, keeping her eyes on the heavenly bodies. "With that much power, I mean. If you could control the dead, surely you could control just about anything."

"I'd take you in my arms and disappear, you know? Make an Eden out there in the middle of nowhere."

Fox laughs. "Are we going to walk around wearing leaves and talking to snakes?" She takes my hand and presses her finger tips against mine.

"Well, I mean, yeah I suppose we could put on leaves if we were dressing up for something." I wink and kiss the back of her hand.

"Sounds like a cool plan, babe. You should go back to magic school and learn that one."

I almost fall off the roof laughing. "I've barely got enough ability to tie my own shoes without my hands. A full-blown fantasy world is probably not in the making for me even in our lifetimes."

Fox sits up and pats me on the leg. "Well, then I guess we'll have to make it happen for ourselves. And that requires money. Which means we are heading to Necrotown." She snatches the bottle out of my hand, takes a swig, and climbs back through the window. "You coming?"

Reaching in, I steal the bottle back and swallow as much as the tank'll hold. I'm going to need it. "I guess so."

Back in the apartment, I finally figure out which damn pocket I hid my smokes in, and we are almost to the car by the time I find the lighter in my shirt pocket. Go figure. Two cigarettes, one for me and one for the lady, and we are on our way.

Necrotown: Mountain City Chronicles

There's no quick route through the Glow to Necrotown. The dead kids' territory butts up to the Glow, but since no one goes there, the city didn't bother extending the highway that far south. They probably figure the more creeps they can keep in the Glow and Necrotown and out of Downtown, the better.

I lean my seat back and close my eyes. There's nothing new to see, riding through the ghetto. Just wasted time, wasted inhabitants, wasted life, and I should know, I'm the king of wasted lives.

Something slams against the hood of the car and sends me bolt upright.

"Pull the fuck over," an angry black man is shouting at us. "We gotta talk about some shit." Dexter points at an empty parking lot.

Fox turns the car into the lot. I would guess it's a matter of confusion, not any fear over what Dexter might do to either of us. I open the door of the car and step on something rubber and squishy. I hate this town. Finish the job and split for the beach—that's the plan.

I hop on the hood of the car and light another smoke as Dexter comes stomping our way. "You've got some nerve showing back up in my corner of town." He wags his finger at us. If ol' Dex had any magical juice, I'd be worried as worked up as he is.

"Whoa, whoa, whoa, buddy." Fox holds up her hands. "What the hell has gotten into you?"

"Word is all over about one bloody fucking hotel room. People are saying there's a couple folks turned up dead and more people are saying Jimmy the blood dealer is one of them. I oughta turn your asses into the cops. You was looking for Jimmy, now he's dead."

I blow out a puff of smoke. "C'mon, Dex, don't act like the cops care about anything that happens here."

Dexter's eyes flare.

"Tell me this, did five-oh even bother putting police tape around the crime scene?"

Silence.

"Hell, did they even bother calling an ambulance to take the bodies away?"

Dexter's jaw flairs. He clicks with his tongue. "You know the answer well as I do. But you know what Dexter had to do? He had to take Jimmy the blood dealer's body home to his mother, his poor fucking neck broken like some sick puppet. Did you do that to him?" Dexter has a revolver aimed at me in a blink.

The weight of my gun presses against my back. I could make a move, Fox can read me enough to get out of the way, but I don't want to rush things. Dexter's no killer. Let's see where this goes.

"We didn't kill Jimmy, Dex."

"Fuck you didn't. Who did then?" Dexter's forearm flinches as his finger tightens on the trigger. I could be wrong.

"Bloodmonger," Fox says.

"Bloodmonger?" Dexter laughs so hard it echoes in the alley. He steps closer—bad move—and presses the gun against Fox's chest. "Are you sure that's the answer you want to go with?"

In less than the time it takes me to get angry about this low life magic peddler touching my wife, she has disarmed him, pistol-whipped him, and effectively wiped the smug clean off of his person. On all fours, he spits teeth and blood into a puddle of something in the parking lot. Fox opens the clip, dumps the bullets onto the ground. She spins the cylinder, flicks it back into place, and drops the weapon in front of Dexter.

"Cut the shit, Dexter. If you have something to say about Bloodmonger, say it." Fox sends one sneaker-clad foot into the side of Dexter's cheek for good measure.

93

"Ah, fuck, okay." Dexter rolls to a sitting position. "But if you really want to know, it's better if I just show you. You aren't going to beat my ass if I stand up, yeah?"

"No games?" I flick my cigarette into the puddle with Dexter's blood. The thing flashes and sends a purple flame eight feet up. Probably a good thing for Dexter—never a good idea to leave bodily fluids or parts in easy access of Mages. They do weird shit with DNA.

"No games," Dexter confirms.

"This better be good."

"Trust me," Dexter says with a laugh, "y'all are gonna shit when you see this."

Chapter 9

Dexter leads us around the corner to an apartment building. The brick dwelling rises six stories with a metal fire escape running up the side and boarded windows every ten feet. Light shines between the cracks of some of the boards. Dogs bark on one of the upper floors. A baby wails from closer to ground level. The building looks like it's one domestic disturbance away from collapse.

"You live here, Dex?" I follow Dexter down a set of stairs that lead below ground level.

"In this shithole? Fuck no." Dexter sticks a key in a doorknob and puts his shoulder into it. "But I own the basement. It's a good place for storing stuff. You know, the stuff I don't want nowhere near where I lay my head at night."

A whiff of the musty stench of death billows out from inside the room.

Fox buries her nose in the crook of her elbow. "Like what, bodies?"

Dexter tugs his shirt up over his nose and mouth. "Ha. You should be ones to talk about bodies. They said that hotel had two stiffs. Witnesses say a flashy redhead split right before they found the bodies."

I take shallow breaths with my mouth, trying not to inhale the graveyard stink. "We told you, that wasn't us."

"Stick with your story, huh? That's cool. I can respect that, but you're still full of shit." Dexter flips on the lights.

A handful of bulbs hanging from century-old wiring illuminate the space. Concrete ground, brick walls, a few questionable puddles of liquid on the floor, nothing special.

A groan echoes in the corner.

"What was that?" I separate my feet, ready to fight.

Another groan. A figure stumbles out from behind one of the brick pillars supporting the foundation. The man looks more eighties than the entire cast of Lost Boys put together. Torn leather jacket (probably has a Misfits skull patch on the back), skinny jeans (or it could just be acid wash body paint for as tight as they are), a weird mullet Mohawk combo, and a silver cross earring hanging off his left lobe. "Whaumpfph."

"A fucking Bloody Shambler?" Fox's voice is muffled from behind her elbow.

The Shambler takes a step forward. His jaw hangs slack, but his eyes are wide open. The Shambler's stare flits from Fox to me to Dexter. His eyes might take things in, but nothing is making it to his brain.

Shambler's have no soul. They happen when someone like Fox pushes their soul out and then leaves. Fox is a rare breed though. I've never met anyone like her operating in Mountain City. The last time someone hired me to track and kill a Kitsune, I ended up married to the fox.

Only one other group is trademarked for Bloody Shambler activity, the Necros. Bloodmonger has a long history of trying his dead magic on people and doing little more than separating their soul from their body. This must be another Necro reject.

The Shambler locks his gaze on Dexter. The zombie screams. Drags his feet a step closer. Intricate tattoos are inked along its jaw line. Some of them are dead magic-symbols. Skulls mixed with never-ending knots. Supposed to mean something about eternal death and eternal life in harmony or some bullshit. I never made it that far into regular magic, let alone Necro magic.

"So who is this poor fucker?" The wicked smell parks on my tongue. I rub it against the roof of my mouth, trying to scrub the gross away. I gag and put my shirt over my mouth.

Dexter bursts out with laughter. He hunches over and slaps his knee. "You don't know? You're going to blame shit on him and you don't even know?"

"Wait. This is Bloodmonger?" Fox moves toward the Shambler, reaches out to touch him.

The zombie snarls, but doesn't do anything. They don't eat brains or flesh. They are after souls. Only problem—problem for them, anyway—they don't possess any of the magic required to take a soul. Bloody Shamblers are creepy and kind of sad, but they aren't even the slightest bit dangerous.

"Yes, you stupid fucks. This is Bloodmonger." Dexter slaps Bloody Shambler Bloodmonger on the back. "So do you want to tell me now why you killed Jimmy?"

Fox traces a finger down Bloodmonger's cheek. The zombie rubs against her touch like a cat. I catch an expression on her face I can't place. Pity, maybe? Fox doesn't bring her past up much, and I told her I would never ask, but from time to time she gets drunk and talkative.

One night over a couple packs of cigarettes and a fifth of bourbon, she told me about how in her younger years she left a trail of Shamblers in her wake. If she saw a body she wanted, she took it. Bounced around city to city, taking bodies and leaving Shamblers behind.

She has the power to share a body with its host soul, but it takes a lot of power and she was young. She wanted to have fun, not fight for control. So instead of sharing, she gave the boot to the hosts, leaving behind a wake of displaced souls.

That night, she fell asleep on my chest. It killed me to watch the sadness in her eyes as she told me the story, but what's done is done. All I could do was hold her and remind her that tomorrow is another day. She's been in the same body since she met me. Fuck the cynics; people can change if they want.

Fox turns from Shambler-Monger. "We didn't kill Jimmy, Dexter."

"Well, who did? And this time don't blame it on this dope. I've kept him locked up in my basement for a week now."

"We don't know," I say. "There was an old corpse in the hotel room, looks like a Hair killed it a week or so ago and buried it in the mattress. Someone possessed the dead body and killed Jimmy. Then whoever it was, took over dead Jimmy's body, too. The pair of corpses attacked us, so we split."

Dexter rubs a hand over his head. "Any idea who was pulling the strings on the Deadman marionettes?"

"Nope." Fox takes my hand in hers. "Magic that powerful, we assumed it had to be someone with juice. The Necro leader seemed like a great starting place. Apparently, we were wrong."

"Man, the Necros are a bunch of fuck ups, magical rejects. Y'all know that. Everyone knows that."

"Who the hell else is going to be possessing corpses?" I ask, not ready to volunteer any information on Sarah.

Dexter stares at Bloodmonger. "I don't know. There've been rumors floating around. Rumors of some chick—everyone said she was Bloodmonger's girl. Some raven-haired jailbait, they said."

"You know her name?" I grab a pen to write a name I already know. There's no need to tell Dexter until necessary.

"Nope. Rumors are wind like that. They're never solid, just words that breeze through the ghettos." Dexter wiggles his fingers to symbolize wind or the existential crisis of man or some shit.

"That's real poetic, Dex." I put my pen away. "Any other, more solid, rumors about what's going down in Necrotown?"

"With Bloodmonger missing, the Necros have to be uneasy," Fox says. "Any of them ventured up this way?"

"That's the weirdest part." Dexter walks toward the door. "No one's heard shit from the Necros. They've been even quieter than usual. Not a peep out of the creepy fuckers in weeks."

The Glow has a tense relationship with the Necros. The deal is, they stay at the bottom of the city and no one fucks with them. The Necros usually follow the deal within reason, but occasionally someone in the Glow goes missing. No one important. A hooker here, corner drug dealer there. The Necros have never been caught snatching people, but everyone knows who does it.

"Has anyone gone there to see why it's so quiet?" I tug at Fox's hand to bring her out of the basement.

Dexter shuts the door, locks Bloodmonger inside. "Because everyone is jumping up and down to go there and ask questions? Fuck that. They're minding their own, for once. Whatever happened there can stay there for all I'm concerned."

"So why show us the body?" Fox takes out a pair of cigarettes from her pocket and lights them. She gives one to me and burns through half of hers in one long drag. The smoke does wonders for cleaning out the smell of a Bloody Shambler.

"Because I didn't want you to go blaming what happened to Jimmy on our friend down there. The last thing I want is people gearing up to go to Necrotown on a witch hunt."

"So what are you going to tell everyone happened to Jimmy?" Fox drops her cigarette on the concrete, rubs it out with her sneaker.

Dexter jogs up the stairs, back to street level. "I'm going to tell everyone I don't know what happened, but the redhead that fled the scene sounds suspicious as all hell."

I blow out a long stream of smoke. "Gee, Dex, thanks," I yell up after the petty magic peddler.

Dexter leans over the railing to look on me and Fox. "Ah, you two will be all right."

"You read that in some chicken bones?" I drop my smoke on the ground next to Fox's.

"No. Y'all are both practically immortal, what's the worst anyone can do to you?"

"Rebirth hurts like a bitch, you know." I shout, but Dexter is gone, off to peddle magic supplies like a dealer sending out meth.

"I suppose I should keep my head low for a little while." Fox grabs another pair of cigs. Sune has crept up her arm and sniffs at the smoke. The fox stays close to the smoke. I wonder if it can smell the body, too.

"Probably. On the bright side, this place has a short memory for petty crimes like murder. How many people could have possibly given a shit about a blood dealer like Jimmy?"

Fox takes a drag from her smoke. "Hopefully not many."

"So what now?" I say, thinking out loud. Bloodmonger showing up soulless in a basement kind of shoots down the whole 'going to talk to Bloodmonger' plan.

"Same as ever. We go to Necrotown and see what's going on."

"With their leader hanging out in there?" I point at the basement door. "Do you really think now is a good time to be a stranger in Necrotown?"

"Who said I'm a stranger?" Fox puts her back to the basement door. She takes a look up at the street. No one in sight. Fox brings her leg forward and drives her heel back into the shitty door. The frame cracks, but doesn't open. One more stiff kick does the job.

"I don't know if I like where you're going." I follow her into the basement, flip on the light.

"You said it yourself, it's not safe to be a stranger down there right now." Fox whistles.

Bloody Shambler Bloodmonger staggers out from behind the same brick column as earlier. He drags himself over to her. She rubs her thumb across his cheek, smiles at the poor, soulless bastard. Sune moves to her forearm, across her fingers and on to Bloodmonger's cheek.

I step forward to catch Fox's now soulless body as she collapses. I drag her lifeless body over to the column and lean her against it so she's hidden from view.

Bloody Shamblers move and moan because of their former souls. For whatever reason, an echo of themselves stays behind, keeps the body animated. Eventually, that echo fades and so do the Shamblers. The soul that inhabited Fox's body has been gone for a long time, there is no echo left to keep the body moving. The body I know and love stays leaned up against the brick, still as a comatose patient.

I will never get used to this sight. Just the idea of losing her sends a chill up my spine. Before Fox, I was nothing. With her gone, I would go right back to that. My fingers rub up against the scars on my forearm that run from wrist to elbow.

"Hey, you okay?" Bloodmonger's hand closes on my shoulder.

I flinch. Fox/Bloodmonger had completely faded from my brain for a minute. "Yeah, Fox, I'm good. Let's get this over with. You're much sexier with a c-cup and without a mullet."

BloodFox smiles. The silver cross earring sways side to side. "Come on then." She walks out the door.

I follow and pull the door shut, doing my best to position it in a way that doesn't look like it's just been kicked in. When I'm done I turn around and BloodFox is gone. "What the fuck?"

I jog up the stairs, and the streets are empty. The dark presses in on me. My chest tightens. Where the fuck is she?

A car pulls to the curb. The passenger window drops, and BloodFox leans over from the driver seat. "Need a lift?"

I open the door and get in a Toyota Tercel. The bottom of the dash is ripped open. A couple exposed wires are twisted together, car-jacker style. The car is at least as old as Fox's, but the owner has kept it in mildly better shape. BloodFox punches the accelerator before I have my door closed.

"You scared the shit out of me." I buckle my seatbelt. Like it matters. If we get in a wreck in this thing we'll die. When they built this car, car manufacturers' idea of safety was an in-dash ashtray.

"What's the matter? Afraid of the Glow at night?" BloodFox winks at me.

Although Fox and Bloodmonger both wear the same amount of mascara, the gesture does not, I repeat, does not translate across both bodies.

I shiver. "Please never do that again."

BloodFox jerks the wheel to the left. The tires squall as they point down the main drag to Necrotown.

Here we go. I fucking hope she can sell this.

Chapter 10

BloodFox drives the old Toyota straight out the asshole of Mountain City and directly into the toilet. The old buildings and bright lights of the Glow get shabbier and shabbier until we pass a block consisting solely of broken foundations. After the empty block, we drive through a small abandoned park. The park is the official border between Necrotown and the rest of Mountain City. Everyone knows not to go south of the park unless they have a death wish.

Or a death obsession.

The park is nothing but a row of cypress trees that reach up to almost touch the full moon hanging low in the sky tonight. The breeze from the car passing by makes the branches tremble like a blob of pine-needle-flavored Jell-O. We break through the park and enter Necrotown.

There's not a sign.

No marker.

No parade announcing, 'Welcome to our fine corner of the city.'

There is nothing. Well, nothing other than shacks and huts and tents pitched like it's goddamn Bonnaroo. The dwellings range from 'that came out of a dumpster' to 'that is a dumpster.'

I drum my fingers against my thigh. Everything about this plan is completely fucked. "Are you sure you can come off as Bloodmonger?"

Fox can take over Bloodmonger's body, but that doesn't automatically give her his knowledge, way of speaking, or mannerisms. She still has to masquerade as the head of a necromaniac cult.

BloodFox sets a hand on my thigh. A tattoo of a snake runs from the back of his hand, around his thumb, across his palm, and back up between his middle and ring finger. Having the head Necro's palm on my leg does not have the comforting effect Fox was probably hoping for.

"What's the matter?" he says. She says? I'm not even sure what pronoun a situation like this calls for. "You don't trust me?"

"Of course I trust you, Fox."

"Bloodmonger. You have to think of me as Bloodmonger while I'm in this body. Otherwise we risk blowing our cover."

"Right, Bloodmonger, of course I trust you. It's just, I don't know, this place creeps me out."

BloodFox slaps her hand on my thigh. "Just follow my lead, don't speak unless spoken to, and don't look anyone in the eye. We'll be fine."

"How do you know so much about this place?"

"A girl can have her secrets, right?"

"A guy."

BloodFox cocks her head to the side, earring touching her shoulder. "Huh?"

"You're Bloodmonger, remember? A guy can have his secrets."

"Well…" Even through all the goth makeup, BloodFox's cheeks show red. "Let's not get too into character yet. We'll just try not to slip up in front of witnesses."

The tents grow more dense the farther south we travel. A forest outline appears on the horizon. The trees signal the official end of Mountain City. There's nothing beyond but woodland for the next two hundred miles, with maybe one or two gas stations to break up the scenery.

The trees seem to grow taller as we approach. "Do you know where you're going?"

"There." BloodFox points.

A building stands at the edge of the tree line. Not a tent or lean-to or shanty, but an actual building made of brick and mortar. As we get closer, the building's shape becomes clearer in the night. The rectangular establishment looks like it was once a library or small community center. No telling what it is now.

Flaps on tents move aside and eyes stare out of the darkness. Beady little eyes with bad intentions and worse magic. If these heathens have finally gotten a strong piece of mojo…I shudder again. Focus back on the building.

BloodFox parks behind a black El Camino. The corpse of a rather large buck hangs off the tailgate of the car. Blood drips from a slice on the animal's neck to a large pewter bowl on the ground.

Fuck this place.

I close my eyes. Just think about Burgess' money. Think about Fox in a teeny, red bikini. Think about mojitos and restaurants and more mojitos. Doing this job for Burgess sucks, but if the old crag is anything, it's well-paid. He'll make sure we get taken care of for this job. We just have to get through it. Find the girl, take her home. No problem, right?

I open the car door, hoping to get a breath of fresh air. Instead, the atmosphere is a pungent miasma of rot. My nose crunches up on its own accord and I cough into my hand. I'd forgotten the smell of this place. If only I could forget the whole god forsaken place.

BloodFox gets out next, walks toward the door of the library-looking building. Every ounce of Fox is gone. BloodFox's walk is completely different, more of a drunken stagger than Fox's usual strut. She's got one hand on her crotch and flicks a zippo lighter open and closed with her other. "Come on, let's get inside." BloodFox's voice is an octave and a half higher. She sounds like the squeak of a pubescent teenage boy, the one all the other kids call 'Screech.'

The change makes me stop for a moment just to watch her. Is this how Bloodmonger acts? I've never actually seen the head Necro. And as far as I know, Fox hasn't either.

Around us, other people—creatures, more like—emerge from their 'homes.' Each of them has on more leather than bodyweight. None of them have on much leather. A jacket here. Chaps there. One woman, all ribs and thigh-gap, wears only a leather police cap. Some of the Necros have on more makeup than an entire Miss America pageant. Others wear only open wrist wounds. The entire group creeps toward us. Some walk, others crawl on hands and feet.

"Creepy as fucking ever," I say.

BloodFox tosses a piece of gum in her mouth, smacks it in her teeth a few times. "Yeah-ha." She smacks me on the chest. "Come on, let's see what's inside." She giggles and staggers to the door.

"This can't be over soon enough," I mutter. I follow BloodFox through the door.

The gutted interior of the building is as desolate as any abandoned warehouse. Whatever it was before—library, community center, whatever—the building could barely even be called an airport hanger now. No walls, no rooms, just an open space. In the middle of the room, the floor has been broken and dug up, leaving a pit. The ceiling has been cut away. A steel beam with shackles attached is mounted above the pit.

"Ay, yo," BloodFox says. "Anybody home?"

To the side of the pit is a makeshift throne. Throne is a bit of a stretch. This is more like a chair made from bones. There's no telling what kinds of bones went into the macabre sculpture. At the end of each armrest is a human skull, and at the top of the back is a deer skull, twelve point antlers reaching up to the roof. Etchings mar the bones with spells, wards, and all sorts of nasty magic. It would be nasty magic if it worked, that is.

A small form steps out from behind the throne, but a black cloak hides the person from view. Moonlight casting through the hole in the ceiling is the room's only illumination. Necros aren't much for electricity, apparently. The Necro moves forward with silent steps.

"Why are you in my home?" BloodFox asks in that same high-pitched voice.

The Necro laughs. The sound is a feminine tinkle, like chimes of glass. "This stopped being your home when I put you out of it to reclaim my rightful place." The Necro sits on the throne and crosses one leg over the other, revealing a black, lacy ballet flat on a slender foot. "Come to think of it, I seem to remember shoving you out of your home and your body at the same time. That makes me wonder just who is standing before me right now."

"I found my way back to my body, bitch," BloodFox says, keeping with the charade.

The door to the building opens. A young man with a skull tattoo that takes up his entire torso steps inside. "Do you require our assistance, Madame?"

A pale hand emerges from inside the robe, waves the man away. "Wait outside. I will call if I require assistance." The Necro rests her palms on the skulls at the armrests. Boney fingers trace over a spell on the right skull.

The tattooed Necro stares hard at us. His gaze freezes on the gun tucked in my waistband. "Are you sure, Madame?"

107

"If I need you, I will call," the woman on the throne says, an edge in her voice. "But I'm sure Sam and Fox Flint will be personally peaceable. Or at least I'm assuming that's you in there, Fox."

Fuck.

So much for the element of surprise.

Fuck.

The Necro bows out of the room after one final glare at us.

"How do you know our names?" I ask.

"I did a little research after our… confrontation. The dead talk, and my, my do they ever have a lot to say about the two of you. The Flints have racked up quite the body count in their days. I'm impressed my Lloyd picked a couple assassins to come find me." The girl slides the hood off her head, revealing the face of a teenage girl. Black hair frames a long face, and dull green eyes bore into us.

Sarah Roswell.

"Yup, that's us," I say, "a couple stone-cold killers out to pick up a bounty."

Between my scruffy-ass and Fox's air of badassery, that statement should have been intimidating. Sarah laughs. Maybe not a holly, jolly knee-slapper laugh, but a definite scoff of unimpressed-ness.

"Go home." Sarah flicks her fingers like she's shooing away a fly that's bothering her.

"Your father told us to bring you home, and that's what I aim to do."

The girl grins, but she breaks it into another snicker. "His *daughter* is gone. You go tell him that."

"Look, kid, I don't know what your problem is, but you need to get off your throne and come with us." BloodFox sounds like Fox again. No point in keeping up the act.

Sarah stands from her throne of bone and moves toward us. I close my hand around my snub-nose. To my right, I hear the familiar flick of one of BloodFox's blades. Sarah doesn't slow. She continues until she's toe-to-toe with me.

"Tell Lloyd that I am gone." Sarah takes my hand and places it against her chest.

Her skin is ice cold.

"What the fuck are you doing?" BloodFox's knife is pressed up against the side of Sarah's neck.

The girl doesn't flinch. She smiles at BloodFox in an amused sort of way. "It's okay, honey, you can feel, too." Sarah places BloodFox's free hand against the side of her neck.

"Oh, shit," BloodFox says.

So, it's not just me then. Because I'd be lying if I said I wasn't having a hard time finding Sarah's pulse.

"Like I said. I'm gone." She steps back, and I'm glad to not be touching her morgue-locker-cold skin anymore.

Is she dead?

"Doesn't matter," I say in a moment of poverty-inspired resolve. "Lloyd paid us to bring you back, we will bring you back."

"Is that why you did this? Just for the money?" Sarah frowns.

The stench of dead magic breezes past me as Sarah draws it in from the air. After the hotel, I want no part of this. I draw my gun.

BloodFox must be equally uneasy. With a flick of the wrist, she sends a switchblade flying in Sarah's direction. The blade thunks into the skull of a skeleton, hovering just in front of Sarah's heart. I have no idea where the skeleton came from.

Sarah pushes her hand forward. The skull with the knife buried in it sails toward Fox. Fox leans to the side, avoiding the macabre baseball. The rest of the skeleton appears behind BloodFox. In one motion it yanks the knife free from the skull and slices it across the back of BloodFox's knee. BloodFox drops to the ground with a shriek of agony. The skeleton plants a knee on her chest and presses the knife against her cheek.

"I asked you a question." Sarah is back in front of me.

She stands a full head shorter than me, and her green eyes are staring so deep into mine I'd swear she was looking into my soul.

"Yes," I say, not sure what answer she wants right now.

"I should kill you. You won't go away, and I'm never going with you. What's stopping me from killing you right now?"

I spread my arms. "Go for it."

She scoffs. "You'd just come right back to life."

"Maybe," I say. "Or maybe this is my time and I'll be gone forever. Maybe you can kill an Immortal. I bet that'd add to your death magic."

"That's it? You would die right here just to look tough?" The right side of Sarah's lip curls to somewhere up around Cincinnati. "You disgust me, Samuel Flint. Get away from me."

The skeleton on top of Fox drops into pieces like a Dry Bones that's just taken one to the head.

"I should kill you for cutting my wife," I say.

BloodFox is on the ground, hands pressed into the back of her knee to stop the bleeding.

"I'm sure your wife has her pretty little redheaded body waiting for her return. I cut a vessel and a dead vessel at that. That body belongs to me more than her anyway."

"Just get me the fuck out of here," BloodFox says.

I scoop her up in my arms. We retreat to the car to lick our wounds and re-evaluate our plans before Sarah changes her mind.

Chapter 11

I drive the car up onto the sidewalk in front of Dexter's stash-pad. On the bright side, it's so late that it's early. A warm light to the east signals the sun's impending ascension. Morning means the streets of the Glow are empty. Everyone has returned home to nurse last night's hangovers.

BloodFox slings open her door and hobbles out. She used a ripped piece of my shirt to tie around her leg on the car ride, but the bandage is doing little more than slowing the blood flow. We need to get her back into her body, ASAP. Even for a Necro, she looks pale.

The door to Dexter's basement is wide open. "Fuck." I run down the stairs, BloodFox limping close behind. How much worse can our luck get?

I race to the column where we left Fox and find it empty. No body. Nothing.

"Goddammit." BloodFox punches the brick. "I liked that body."

"Who in the fuck steals a body?" I grab my hair in my hands, trying not to imagine what someone might do with an unconscious woman.

"A mob. That's who." Dexter stands in the entrance to the basement.

I rush across the room, grab Dexter by the shirt, drive him into the wall. "Where is she?"

"She's right behind you in that body she stole, remember?"

I drive a knee into Dexter's lower stomach. "I've had a shit night. Don't fuck with me, Dexter." Spit flies off my lips. Dexter cringes away, but I grip his shirt tighter. "What did you do with Fox's body?"

"Me? Nothing." Dexter puts up his hands. An innocent angel.

I draw my fist back.

"Whoa. I didn't do anything with her. But someone may have stumbled across an open door. That same someone may have found an unconscious redhead fitting the description of the suspect in Jimmy's murder. They may have come to me, asked questions."

"What did you tell them?" I shake Dexter. I swear to every god in existence if anything happened to Fox, I will kill him.

"What was I supposed to say? I told them she must have broke into my basement and hid down there."

BloodFox's fist comes out of nowhere. Knuckles clash with cheekbone. Cheekbone loses. "What did they do with my body?"

"You know how things work in the Glow. The street has its own style of justice. Believe it or not, people liked Jimmy. They needed a scapegoat for his murder. Sorry, lady, you're the scapegoat." Dexter shrugs. "Not like you can't just hijack another body."

BloodFox punches Dexter again. This shot is to the temple. Dexter drops to the floor, out cold.

"Shit. Now we don't know where they took your body."

"I know where they took it." BloodFox wobbles out the door. "We've got till sunrise."

I chase BloodFox eastward on the empty streets. Well, chase is an unfair word, more like follow at the leisurely pace of someone who's taken a knife to the leg. The orange glow of the upcoming sunrise grows warmer with every bloody step.

"Fox, what are we chasing here?"

BloodFox speeds up, getting every ounce of performance out of Bloodmonger's broken body. "We're chasing daylight."

"I caught that. What happens at sunrise?"

"Executions are always carried out at sunup."

Oh.

Oh, shit. The locals have Fox's body. They think she killed Jimmy. At dawn this crazy bunch of Glow motherfuckers are going to hang Fox's soulless body.

BloodFox grabs a streetlamp and swings herself around a left-hand corner. The sidewalk leads to an open block that used to serve as a city park. Now, the giant area is a dead-grass covered flea market of sorts. The market table tops have all been folded away.

All except for one.

A single table sits in the middle of the square. Atop that table, Fox's body stands with a rope tied around her neck. The rope is strung over a broken out streetlight above the table. An aura of orange magic surrounds Fox. Probably some Mage using his power to keep her comatose body upright.

"Fuck," BloodFox says under her breath. She races into the crowd, pushing and shouldering her way past onlookers.

Everyone loves a public execution.

"Excuse me, pardon me, ah-hem, move." I try my best to follow BloodFox through the swarm of people.

"Hey." BloodFox jumps onto the table with actual Fox. "You have the wrong idea," she says to the crowd. "This woman is innocent."

The crowd boos and shouts muddled obscenities. A dead rat smacks against BloodFox's chest.

Where in the hell did someone find a dead rat?

"Who the fuck are you?"

"That's that goddamn Necro."

"What's he doing this far north?"

BloodFox puts her hands up, a call for silence. "I've come to proclaim the innocence of this woman. She didn't kill Jimmy."

"Well who did?" a faceless voice in the crowd shouts.

"I did." BloodFox points at her chest. "I paid for O neg, and that stingy little bastard sold me AB, like I wouldn't know. You don't fuck with the Necros. I taught him that."

"Bullshit." A different voice this time. A woman's voice.

"Why admit it?" The hoarse voice of an older man.

"Because," BloodFox turns to look at Fox's body. A tear runs down BloodFox's cheek. "I-I love her. I can't see her die over something I did. We were both in the hotel room that night, but I'm the one who killed him."

A low group whisper consumes the crowd. The act is so genuine, I almost feel bad for BloodFox.

After a few hushed moments, I cup my hands around my mouth, shout, "That's the man. I saw him running from the hotel the other night."

The crowd murmur grows.

I move through the crowd. From a different position, I pitch my voice deeper. "Are you going to hang that hottie or a good for nothin' Necro?"

The low buzz cranks up to eleven. Orange magic moves up the rope. The noose lifts from Fox's neck and hangs over BloodFox's. BloodFox juts out her chin. She reaches out, takes Fox's hand. A sign of solidarity.

Or something like that.

The fox tattoo creeps down BloodFox's arm.

The crowd pushes in tighter as I edge my way closer to the table, ready to grab Fox and split.

"You crazy fuckin' Necro, we sentence ya to death," a voice calls.

The group shouts louder. The rope creaks as three large men pull, lifting Bloodmonger's soulless body into the air. With all eyes on Bloodmonger, Fox climbs off the table. I take her—the hot, porcelain skinned Fox—away from the park as fast as I can.

"That was close," I say when we're two blocks away from the redneck gallows.

"Too close." Fox pushes a stray strand of hair out of her face with her free hand.

We finish our sprint to her car and slide in. The car is started and peeling rubber before Bloodmonger's dead body stops twitching.

I give the park a wide berth as I make my way out of town. No need to risk the locals wanting dessert and going back after Fox's neck. I hop on the first side road that leads to our office.

There is, predictably, no parking at our office. I drop Fox off at the front door. We are away from the lynch mob, but we can't be too safe. Fox closes her door and leans in the window. "Be careful out there."

"I'm not the one with rope burns on my neck."

Fox's hand drift up, rubs at the red ring around her throat. "You're never more alive than when you're about to die, right?" She smiles, but the warmth isn't quite there. I'm not sure which of us she's trying to convince.

"Just get inside and keep your head down, babe. I'll be up in a minute."

"Yes, dear." Fox blows me a kiss and disappears into the building.

Never again will I let her leave her body lying around. Next time, we're sticking her in the trunk. Better yet, there won't be a next time. I'm going to park, go home, take a nap, and then we're leaving for the beach. Doesn't even matter which one. Just some beach, somewhere.

Nearest free parking space is a whole block to the east, next to a bazaar that sells samurai swords, World War II memorabilia, and bongs. Hell, probably all sorts of other things to fill the glass bowls with, too. I wouldn't know. I went through my drug phase long before the little shop stoners showed up.

The walk/jog home takes forever. Or at least it feels like it lasts an eternity. Funny how time does the exact opposite of what you want. 'If only this moment could last a little longer,' you wish, and father time says, 'screw you, it's tomorrow already. And you're late for work.'

I sprint up the stairs and into our room. Fox is in bed, wrapped in more blankets than there are in all of Alaska. It's been one hell of a day. Sweat rolls down my forehead. Alive for countless lives, and I'm still in terrible shape. I need a shower.

Fox moves and moans under her blanket mountain. That's it, I'm sold. The shower can wait for later. I drop my clothes and climb into bed with her. It takes all of ten seconds before I can't hold my eyes open any longer. Sleep comes quick and engulfs me like a fire.

Necrotown: Mountain City Chronicles

Chapter 12

Wood splinters. That's an odd sound. With a crash, wood breaks. Something thumps against a wall. I'm instantly awake and reaching for my gun. My fingers wrap around the handle of my snub nose, and I swing around, aiming into pitch black. We must have slept through the day. The question is who the fuck is in my house?

I blink, trying to adjust my eyes. Fox grunts. Something big shrieks. I feel a presence before I see it. The attacker comes from my left. A bulky body, too big to be human, crashes into my shoulder. The gun goes off by reflex, lighting the room. Just long enough to catch sight of three Trolls before I'm night blind again. I try to get the gun between me and the Trolls, but a giant hand slaps the weapon away from me.

Judging from the sound, I'd say the gun ends up somewhere beneath the bed. A lotta good it will do me there. I extend my senses, hoping to catch a jackpot store of magic. There isn't any, or at least not enough to make use of. That's part of the reason I loved this place. Until now, anyway.

I close my eyes and wait. A rush of air comes from my right. I duck underneath a punch that could level the Eiffel Tower and counter with an uppercut to the nuts. The Troll lets out an 'oooff,' and I can feel his weight over the top of me as he bends. I drive both my fingers at where his eyes should be. When it's life and death, there's no such thing as honor or courtesy.

My Troll eyeball-guestimating is off and I end up with one finger scraping the Troll's front tooth and the other stuck up his nose. He shrieks and grabs my hand. The pop is deafening as he snaps two, maybe three, fingers on my right hand. That will hurt like hell once the adrenaline dumps.

Hoping the Troll is still in the same place, I swing my shin towards his groin. Mr. Troll isn't as dumb as he looks. He catches my shin and uses both hands to snap my tibia and fibula. Adrenaline or

119

not, the feeling is nothing less than agony. My good leg buckles as pain overwhelms me.

The bed breaks my fall as I bounce off the edge of the mattress and land on the ground. The Troll's footsteps shake the floor as the beast stalks me. He needs money, so they won't kill me. Quasi-Immortal or not, that's a big chance to take. They'll never collect anything from a dead guy.

I, however, have no problem killing this motherfucker.

I reach for my gun under the bed. It's a blind grab in the dark, but luck is on my side. My hand hits the cold barrel of the all-powerful equalizer. Luck, an always finicky bastard, does not stay on my side. The problem is, the gun is in my right hand. The one the Troll crushed into powdered bone inside a skin sack. I can feel the Troll's presence over me, but there's no time to switch hands. No choice but to take a pot shot.

My index finger and thumb are enough to get the gun off the ground. They are not enough to aim accurately and fire. Before I can squeeze off a shot, the Troll takes the gun out of my hand.

Oh, well. That Troll ain't gonna do shit with my gun.

Cold steel presses against my temple.

I hear the shot. See the flash of the muzzle. Even catch a whiff of gun powder before everything goes black.

Chapter 13

Rebirth sucks, but I've been over that so I'll skip the details. The whole thing takes roughly the same amount of time and hurts just as much as the million times it's happened before today.

I gasp. Cool air chills newborn lungs. I cough, punch the floorboard of the house. "Fuck." I yell, trying to expel the adrenaline associated with the process. My body convulses. Convulsions die to shivers. I roll to sitting, knees tucked to my chest.

"Holy shit." I scoot my back against a wall, away from the Troll sitting in my living room, smiling.

The Troll puts his hands up. "Whoa, whoa, Sam. It's me." Sune creeps down the Troll's arm until its face is in the Troll's palm. The fox's lips sneak back in a canine smile. It winks at me. That fox is a shit. The Troll steps to the side to reveal Fox's lifeless body on the floor behind him.

"Fox? Holy shit. What happened?"

The Troll scratches the base of his throat. The oddly feminine gesture is strange in the hands of a giant. "Three of these assholes broke into our house. I stabbed one in the eye, hopped in this body, and used the bastard's strength to snap the other one's neck." TrollFox scratches behind her ear. "Sorry I didn't save you in time. Again."

"It's okay. This saves me from having to recuperate three broken fingers." I flex my right hand, fingers good as new.

TrollFox's eyes go wide. "I have something for you."

I can't help smiling. Only Fox would come to her re-birthed husband in the body of someone else with a gift. "Oh, yeah, what's that?"

TrollFox holds her arms out to the side. "Tah-dah."

"You brought...me, a...Troll?"

"Yup."

"I may be foggy from the whole dying thing, but what the hell do I want with some Troll?"

"Not just *some* Troll." TrollFox claps her hands. "But the Troll who was the triggerman. Or triggertroll. Or whatever."

That is an interesting gift. She knows me so well. "Is he still in there?"

TrollFox rolls her eyes in her head. "He's still in here. He's pissed, too." TrollFox smiles.

When Fox takes over a body she can push the person's soul out or just borrow the body. Looks like she just took this one out on loan.

"Could you, uh, go back to the sexy body? Troll doesn't suit you too well." Fox's gestures on the Troll are freaking me out. I've seen Fox in a few different bodies, but this one is by far the weirdest.

TrollFox curls a shoulder up, goes for a sly grin. It comes out all kind of jumbled. The awkwardness must even be apparent to her. "Fair enough." She shrugs, sets a hand on unconscious Fox's thigh.

Sune moves from the Troll's arm to Fox's leg. The Troll passes out. His head bounces off the wood floor. Fox seamlessly comes to life. She stands. "So what about him?"

I reach out for a loose, warped floorboard. The three-foot long piece of wood has two long nails sticking through the end. "The fucker killed me. I could at least repay the favor."

Fox shrugs, checks the paint on her nails. "Good. I was going to do it if you didn't." She moves to the dresser in the corner of the giant living space. "I'll go get your clothes."

The board is heavy in my hand. The hundred-year-old, half-rusted nails are as menacing as any bullet. Killing is something they say changes a man. In all my years, I have killed and been killed. Any ceremony involved with taking a life is gone.

Three steps close the distance.

Two feet plant for power.

One wide arc gives speed.

Zero remorse.

Two nails bury deep in the temple of the Troll.

The body flinches from the impact.

The floorboards creak as Fox makes her way back. She tosses me a Rise Against t-shirt and pair of jeans that no longer have knees and the back pockets are not long for this world.

I hold the pants up. "Really?"

"Your clothing stores are dying quicker than you are. You don't even want to know what your other choice was. Some things should remain dead—the eighties especially."

"Touché." I dress and put on an identical pair of work boots to the ones I died in. Styles come and styles go, but steel toe is forever.

"What about that?" Fox nods at the Troll's body.

"Did you drive?"

Fox scoffs.

My house is twenty miles from the Glow. Walking isn't exactly an option. "Rebirth, um, clouds my mind? I'm, um, still waking up. Are you in your car?"

"Hell, no. The Troll mafia had an Escalade parked out front, so I jacked that shit." Fox holds up a keychain with a diamond mounted in a leather strap.

Trolls are known for many things. Subtlety has never been one of them.

"So we've got a dead body and a stolen tank. Perfect. Let's throw the body in the trunk and go for a drive." I rip the board free from the Troll's head.

Troll blood, more or less the same as human blood— if human blood was the consistency of syrup—pours onto my floor. I'm not worried. The blood will seep into the floorboards eventually. I only come here when I die, and it's far enough from town to avoid detection.

Fox and I each grab a leg and drag the Troll out the front door. An orange sun droops low in the sky, partially obscured by Moonshine Ridge to the west. The night will help with the next part.

With a three count and a pair of grunts, we heave the Troll into the trunk of the luxury SUV. I close the rear hatch, and super black tint takes care of hiding the body… For now.

Fox brushes dust off her pants. "What's next, babe?"

I eye Moonshine Ridge, all switchbacks and steep cliffs.

A hundred years ago, a High Mage got drunk off his ass on mountain moonshine. Apparently, his girlfriend dumped him for a Sharp. What any woman would see in someone with razor blades in his mouth, I'll never know. Whatever caused it, the Mage stumbled to town in a drunken, angry stupor. It took half the police force of Mountain City, with backup from the Hairs—this was back before the Standards in Mountain City hated the Hairs—to bring the Mage down. Some political types blamed the alcohol and tried to ban the shine.

The plan worked as well as could be expected. The shiners moved higher up the mountains, paid off a few cheap Mages for cloaking spells, and set up shop. With moonshine banned, they could charge a fortune for it. The ban only lasted two years, but some of those shiners' kids are still power players in the city today.

These days, Moonshine Ridge is kind of a tourist attraction. Twenty minute drive north of the city and you get a mouthful of history, or at the very least, a lot of privacy. Old timers come up to share stories, young kids come up to lose their virginity. I'm going up to dump a body. It's a multi-purpose location.

"You still got those keys?"

Fox flashes the keychain. The sparkle of the diamond matches the sparkle of the giant chrome wheels on the vehicle.

"Good. You follow me."

"What are you driving?" Fox gets in the driver's seat of the SUV.

"I've got something special. I store it up here for emergencies."

The lock on the shed is covered in rust, and it takes some effort, but I get the combination in. The lock pops off, and the door creaks open. Metal gardening tools chime against each other as a gust of wind blows through the open door. I shoulder the door to open it wider, let some light in.

Orange light filters through and illuminates the automotive holy grail. A silver 1967 Ford Mustang GT500 stares back at me from inside the shed. The car almost looks pissed to have been left alone for so long. Then again, what muscle car doesn't look angry?

I turn the key to the on position and wait. The dash lights up. It's been at least a decade since I drove this car, but I've tried to keep gas in the tank and the battery charged. Hopefully, there's still enough juice left to start the car. I twist the key. The motor fumbles a few rotations, backfires. "Come on, baby." I twist again. The engine burbles, fills the shed with white smoke.

"Come on. Go, baby, go."

The car dies.

I punch the roof. The top of the car is already dented from the last time the car killed me. Deadman's Curve is more of a plural around these parts. Mountain roads are dangerous in a car with more horsepower than I have brains. I got the car mostly restored back to perfect before I garaged it. The dent in the roof is the only reminder of the rollover. That and bloodstains on the head liner.

I twist the key and hold the pedal to the floor. The engine cranks and roars to life like a pissed off dinosaur. Which is fitting since just starting the car probably burns through a T. rex worth of fossil fuel.

"Hell yeah." I blip the throttle a few times to make sure she'll stay running. When it settles into a smooth idle, I press on the clutch and notch the shifter into first. I ease the car out of the shed. The shocks are stiff and creaky, but the engine runs like a champ. I don't bother closing the shed. If anyone wants to steal fifty-year-old tobacco farming tools, they can have them.

Gravel peppers the old building as I floor it past Fox and out onto the main road. Warm evening air blows through my hair. This car is a kind of freedom I'd forgotten about. Control over this much power is intoxicating. I shift into third, hard, and the back tires bark as they threaten to lose traction. The smile on my face is automatic. It's been too long. I haven't been in this seat since the sixth time this car killed me. It seemed like seven accidental deaths in the same car was pushing my luck, so I garaged it. Although the second and fifth times may have been on purpose.

Tires squall behind me. I need to remember it's tough for Fox to keep up. That SUV may have a motor the size of an aircraft, but nothing like the pony car. I back off to cruising speed and head a few miles up Moonshine Ridge. There are scenic pull-offs peppered along the road for wannabe photographers to pull over and snap pictures. I find a particularly deserted looking one and park. The view looks down on the lights of Mountain City. The place almost looks nice when it's nothing but colored dots in a nighttime landscape.

Fox parks behind me, slams her door. "How have you not told me you have a vintage muscle car parked in your garage? I thought marriages were about honesty. And honestly this is the coolest thing I've seen this week." Fox trails her long fingers across the hood of the car, stopping against the small side mirror.

"Yeah, me and this bad boy go way back. Hasn't always been pretty. I've rebuilt this thing more times than I can count."

"Bad boy?" Fox scoffs. "Look at those curves. This is one bad lady."

I toss Fox the key. "Well, you can drive us home in her when we're done."

She smiles. Her hand is still on the car and Sune has slid down her arm to sniff at the clear-coat.

I open the hatch of the Escalade. "Yup. Still a dead body in there. Help me with him."

Together we load the Troll into the driver seat. Fox buckles him. I start the car, shift into drive, and place the Troll's giant foot on the accelerator. The Escalade kicks up a cloud of dust and it hops the curb and rolls off the side of the mountain.

"You know," Fox says as she watches the vehicle tumble, "when they find that car, they will know the Troll didn't die from the accident. There are two holes in his temple."

"Doesn't matter. If the police investigate, they won't have anything to pin on us. The Trolls won't give us up to them because they can't collect if we get arrested."

"And the Trolls?"

"The Trolls sent those three after us. When they don't come back with our heads, I'm assuming the head honchos will probably put two and two together. Trolls are dumb, but not that dumb. More will be coming."

Fox shrugs. "Sad waste of a car though. That thing had everything but a mini-bar inside it."

I could use a drink. "We need to talk about this mess."

"Yeah, but you'll have to speak up over the engine roar." Fox drops into the front seat of the Mustang.

Once I'm inside, she launches hard and attacks the mountain road at breakneck speed.

"What are we going to do?"

"About which part?" I ask.

"The Trolls. Or Sarah. Or Burgess. Or any of it really." Fox downshifts and powers through a sweeping right-hand corner.

"I don't know."

"Well, I say we leave. There's gas in the tank. Let's just split. You know you want to."

I listen to the throaty exhaust, roll options around in my head. "I don't know if it's that easy."

"Why not?"

"The Trolls broke into our house. Tried to kill us."

"They did kill you."

"Exactly," I say. "That's not normal behavior. Now that we've killed three of their own, I have no idea how far they'll go to track us."

"Screw the Trolls. They can come at us. We can take them."

"Even if we could, there's still Burgess."

"Forget him, too." Fox squeezes the steering wheel hard enough to pop a knuckle.

"He's already paid us. We can't back out now or he'll want his money back."

"He's just one old man. Fuck him."

"He's a rich old man. And he has a whole armada of mercenary Mages he would sic on us in a second."

Fox bites her lip. We drive in silence—as silent as it gets in the interior of a forty-year-old car, anyway—for a few miles. "Fine," she finally says, "what do you suggest we do?"

"We go talk to Burgess. We make sure he wants Sarah back. If he does, we find a way to coax her. His money can buy our freedom. We pay back the Trolls, and then we break for the beach. I've heard good things about St. Augustine."

Ahead a sign warns us of a split in the road. Left goes Downtown and right to the north side of town. Fox clicks on her blinker and follows the road to the right.

"Where are you going? Burgess' office is Downtown."

"If we are going through with this, I need something heavier duty than a switchblade, and you need a step up from that snub nose."

"How are we going to pay?"

"I know a guy," Fox says.

"You know a guy?"

She grins at me. "He's an old...*friend*."

Chapter 14

I keep my grip on the oh-shit handle over the door. Just because the highways in Mountain City are called highways, doesn't mean they are wide and straight. On the upper half of the city, Valley View is a two-lane road with more kinks than the internet.

"I just want you to know that I'm not exactly comfortable up in Hair Nation." I lean over to glance at the speedometer. Although it doesn't literally say 'too fuckin' fast,' it might as well. "And do we need to be doing it at over a hundred miles an hour?"

"I told you, we need big guns." Fox speeds up another five miles per hour. "And it's midnight on an empty road. Good time to stretch the old legs."

"So how do you know a Hair arms dealer?"

"All Hairs are arms dealers, and everyone who lives in the Glow packs heat. Are you telling me you don't know any Hair arms dealers?"

"Not quite. The Hairs and I aren't exactly… close."

"Holy shit, Sam, does anybody like you?"

"You do."

"Like is a strong word."

"We sleep in the same bed every night, naked."

"Lust has nothing to do with liking a person." Fox winks.

I decide she's kidding but drop the subject, just in case she's not.

Necrotown: Mountain City Chronicles

The last couple miles to Hair Nation pass in a literal blur. Fords built while Lyndon B. Johnson was still in office were not meant to grip corners at this speed. There is nothing north of Hair Nation, so the only real marker we've exited the middle of nowhere and entered werewolf territory is a million-year-old willow tree with a claw mark on the north side and a bite taken out of it on the south side. Passing the tree—well, I assume it was the right tree, it passed by pretty quick—puts us in Hairitory.

"Who *exactly* are we going to see?"

"Ethan Grisom. He's the—"

"Biggest arms dealer in Mountain City." I drop my head against the passenger window, forehead thunking against the glass. Its dull throb is nothing compared to the pain I'm about to feel.

"Great. You know him?"

"Vaguely, but he sure remembers me."

Fox takes her eyes off the road to give me a sideways glance. "What does that mean?"

"A couple years before we met, Lloyd Burgess shows up in my office. He didn't look like anything special, but he said he had money and wanted to hire me for proof his girlfriend was cheating on him." I roll my face against the cool glass. "I followed his girlfriend to Hair Nation. She met weekly at a warehouse there. Drove her giant Chevy Suburban in, stayed for thirty minutes, drove right back out."

Fox clutches the wheel in a death grip as she drives toward the very same warehouse.

"So, I snapped a few pictures. I got her car outside the warehouse, dashing Ethan Grisom coming out to open the garage door, and her leaving thirty minutes later. Job well done, right? Yeah, came right around to proper fuck me. The girl wasn't Burgess' girlfriend. She was a Hair runner. The cops had a deal with the Hairs—they can deal all the guns they want as long as they keep them out of Downtown. Well, Ethan and his pals got greedy—they were trucking semi-autos into Downtown like mad. Mountain City Police Department had no idea."

"MCPD doesn't have jurisdiction in Hair Nation, and for that matter, the Hairs make sure they're well paid." Fox makes a turn without silly little things like brakes or blinkers.

"That's why Burgess needed a dope like me. He got my dumb ass to snap the pictures, and then he anonymously sent them to the cops. That's why money-bags Burgess hired a low rent dick to do the work, he didn't want to risk any of his good contacts."

"So, that's the job Burgess burned you on." Fox huffs out a loud breath. The sound could be a tired laugh, but comes across as something else. Something sadder. "Figures."

"Yup. MCPD arrested the runner on her next trip through downtown. Her arrest made the papers. She was a sort of celebrity for the week it took someone to shank her in prison."

"They never found out who did that if I remember correctly." Fox's lips take on a sideways grin.

Too tired to question the grin, I press on. "The police took to the press to say a good Samaritan turned in photographic evidence that proved Ethan Grisom was behind the especially illegal gun running. Add that to Burgess' smear campaign against Ethan and the Hairs, and it made human/Hair relations even shakier. One rat started the race wars we are surrounded by now."

The muscle at the corner of Fox's jaw twitches. "And let me guess, somehow Ethan found out you were the rat."

"Crazy how that worked out, isn't it? Either way, cops put a warrant out for Ethan. They picked him up a couple months later, and he spent another six months behind bars for the charge."

"Ethan's not a bad guy. Maybe he's forgiven you." Fox sets a hand on my shoulder. "Hell, he might not even remember you if it's been that long back."

"Oh, he remembers me."

"What makes you so sure?"

"I've bumped into him four times since then. He's killed me three times."

"Oh." Fox keeps her gaze on the road.

"Luckily, he was quick about it the second and third times. I think I'm mostly just a nuisance at this point."

Fox squeezes my arm. "Don't worry, he won't hurt you with me around." Fox parks in front of the warehouse, kills the engine.

"What makes you so sure?"

Three humongous men and a woman the size of a small refrigerator step out a warehouse door. The largest man walks up to the car. He stares at Fox and his lips part into the wide smile of a jackal.

"Because we used to date." Fox opens her door before I can tell her what a terrible joke she just made.

I grab my spare pistol out of the dash, flip the cylinder open. Three rounds to four Hairs. Yeah, that seems like a proper death sentence. Ethan stares at me through the windshield, teeth barred. This is going to suck. I open my door and tuck the gun in the back of my pants.

Ethan growls. "What are you doing here? Do I need to kill you a fifth time?" His voice isn't so much a threat as a promise of death.

"Technically, you've only killed me three times, Hair-brain. I survived our last encounter, mostly."

Ethan takes a step at me. I grab the gun.

Fox stops Ethan with a hand on his chest. "Take it easy, Ethan, he's with me."

Ethan leers at Fox. "And just who, the fuck, are you?"

"An old friend." Fox holds her arm out to the side. Sune dances across the inside of her arm for Ethan to see.

"Orange Coat?" Ethan stumbles a few steps to the side, catches himself on the hood of the Mustang. Two of the other Hairs stare at Fox's tattoo, faces slack in shock.

The lady Hair snatches Fox by the wrist to examine her tattoo. The fox pretends to lick Lady Hair's hand. Lady Hair shoves Fox's arm away. "This can't be. What kind of trick is this? Fox is dead."

"No trick. It's really me." Fox's voice cracks. She smiles at the Lady Hair. "It's great to see you again, Elsa. You too, Gabriel." Fox nods at an older, blonde Hair standing next to Elsa.

Fox sways, and I wrap her in my arms. I'm not sure what's going on, but I've never seen Fox show emotion around anyone but me. She needs me. Fox hums as she presses against my body.

Ethan stands up from the hood of the car, fists balled and tears in his eyes. I liked him better on TV with a suit and a smile. Unhinged werewolf is not something I want on my plate right now.

Fox stands in front of me. "Ethan, I'd like you to meet Sam Flint."

"I know his name," Ethan growls. His eyes tint yellow. Pupils warp to slits. His salt-and-pepper beard is a quarter-second away from growing into a fearsome black and white mane.

"He's my husband."

135

That stops the Hair in his tracks. Good thing, too. Human form Ethan would kick my ass. Hair form Ethan would rip me to pieces.

Ethan steps back. He runs a hand through a headful of wavy, slicked-back hair. Not done grooming, he rubs both palms against bearded cheeks. "I'm sorry, love, but did you come back from the grave just to introduce me to your new husband?"

"No. We came here because we need your help. *I* need your help."

Ethan glares over Fox's shoulder at me. His fists are still balled into cinderblocks of death. A slight growl continues in the back of his throat.

"Can we talk?" Fox's voice is low, concerned, sincere.

"*We* can talk. *He* can wait outside." Ethan nods at me.

"Fucking hell I will." Like I'm about to let Fox stroll into a dark building with Ethan Grisom.

Fox turns away from the Hair. She leans in close to my ear. "I can handle myself. Do you trust me?"

"Yes." My voice comes out painted in shades of a heart trampled with gravel.

"Good," she whispers. "Wait out here, and I'll be back with enough ammunition to get us the hell out of this godforsaken city."

I hate this so fucking hard.

Do you trust her?

She's my wife, of course I trust her.

Then let her go…

The battling conscience argues another problem to an end I hate. Why does my inner me have to be so much smarter than my outer me?

"Be careful in there." I wrap my arms around Fox and plant a kiss on her lips.

Ethan's growl makes me smile. Fuck that guy.

Fox moves away. Her devious grin says she knows exactly what, or better who, that kiss was for.

"Let's go to my private office. You remember the way, right, my little Orange Coat?" Ethan's turn to play smug.

Bastard.

I count to ten. Still pissed. Twenty. Instead of counting sheep, I'm counting dead Hairs.

The door to the warehouse closes and leaves me locked outside with three Hair bodyguards. All four of us stare at the warehouse.

"So, uh…" I scratch the back of my head. "Anybody got a drink around this place?"

The Hairs exchange a look too brief for me to interpret, but probably enough for a pack to exchange a lifetime of conversation. They have some sort of weird wonder-twin connection like that.

"Fuck it," Elsa says. "If I've got to babysit Sam the Snitch here, I'm going to get lit while doing it."

A younger hair—twenty, maybe—slaps me on the shoulder. "You won't get any ideas and try to shoot us while we get hammered, will you?"

I get the gun, open the cylinder, and drop the three bullets into my palm. The Hairs watch. Electric tension buzzes through the air. I flip the gun closed and toss the younger Hair the bullets. "There, keep that on retainer for as long as you feel necessary."

Gabriel says, "You aren't worried we will try to kill you?"

"If you decided to kill me, would the three bullets in that gun make an ounce of difference?"

Gabriel's turn to smack me on the back. The impact knocks the air out of me.

"I like you," Gabriel says. "I can see why Orange Coat picked you up." He walks to a work truck with more rust than paint parked a few feet away. He drops the tailgate and jumps in the bed.

"What makes you say she picked me up?"

I follow Elsa and the younger Hair to the truck.

"A woman like Fox," Elsa takes a seat on the tailgate, "she sees what she wants and takes it, not the other way around."

I laugh and jump on the tailgate next to her. She has a point. From the moment the stars aligned, luck had it, the universe decided to momentarily stop shitting on Samuel Flint, and Fox decided she wanted me, there was never any other option. She asked me out. She made the first move. She told me I was going to propose. I have always been along for the ride, just trying to hold on tight and not drool on the carpet.

Gabriel opens a metal toolbox and takes out a mason jar filled with transparent yellow liquid.

All the different races have their specialty. Sure, there's whiskey and vodka and gin and all the normal drinks that plain old Standards and supernaturals alike drink. On top of those, everyone's got their thing. Sharps make a cocktail out of bone marrow. Necros have learned how to ferment blood and distill it into rum. The Mages drink champagne laced with magic. No one knows where the magic comes from, and everyone agrees it's probably best not to ask the Mages about it.

Gabriel sits next to me and holds out the jar. I unscrew the lid and the scent ignites in my nostrils like a mini-mushroom cloud of inebriation. I blink back tears.

Drink of choice for Hairs? They call it Deer Piss. Whether or not it contains any actual deer piss remains to be seen. No matter what is inside, the pack of wolves have figured out how to distill it to somewhere around two-hundred fifty proof. Seriously. Someone once tried to use Deer Piss as a Molotov cocktail and lit an entire city block on fire.

"Go ahead, buddy," Gabriel says. "Have a drink."

All three Hairs watch anxiously. All three Hairs have probably underestimated just how little of a damn I give about my senses and my liver. I take a swig out of the jar.

Holy.

Shit.

The.

Burn.

The fire that took over a city block? It's burning my esophagus. I don't flinch. The burn feels good, I embrace it. The alcohol hits my system and, bam, I'm the most level I've been in days.

The Hairs nod approvingly.

"Not too bad for a Standard." Elsa pounds on my back and swipes the Deer Piss.

The impact launches me into a coughing fit. What is it with Hairs and touching people? And side note for all the kids—coughed up Deer Piss is exactly as pleasant as it sounds.

"I'm not a Standard," I spit out when I've caught my breath.

"Can you do magic?" the young Hair asks.

"Not especially well."

"Can you change forms?" Elsa asks.

"Well, no."

"You die and come back to life." Gabriel grabs the jar and has a drink. "Big fucking whoop."

"You're an immortal?" The Young Hair leans in close like he's about to give me a physical.

"Quasi-immortal, technically." I take another drink. Feel even better.

"One of these days he will die, and he won't be coming back," Gabriel says.

"Yeah, but still. Those are rare, like, super rare." Young Hair reaches for the drink in my hand.

Lady Hair swats his hand away and takes the yellow jar. "Not quite, Jordon. You can have some whiskey if you want, but you aren't ready for yellow fire yet."

The kid pouts, kicks at the dirt.

Gabriel swings his legs, the whole truck rocks. "Either way, showing up here with Ethan's dead girlfriend is a good way to get dead, again."

"What's Ethan's problem with you, Sam? You seem like an all right guy." Jordon keeps kicking at the dirt. There's not any whiskey hiding under those rocks.

"It's a long story." The Deer Piss warms my entire body. I passed buzzed somewhere around the time I opened the lid.

"Sammy here fucked Ethan over a few years back." Elsa drinks again.

"I got set up."

"First I've heard of it," Gabriel says.

"If I had told Ethan the truth, would he have believed me?"

"Nope," Gabriel and Elsa say together.

I snatch the glass back out of Elsa's hands, examine the liquid. Half empty means I'm probably fully loaded. So what's another drink? "What's with Fox and Ethan?"

"Oh, shit, story time." Jordon jumps over the side of the truck bed. He lands ass first inside and lays back across the bed liner, staring up at the stars.

Gabriel takes the drink. He stares into the yellow liquid for a long while. "Not a lot to tell. Ethan and Orange Coat were tight way back when. Everyone had more or less accepted the two of them would end up married."

"And then?" I try to imagine Ethan and Fox together. A view of my wife pressed against the rock hard chest of the Hair flashes in my mind. I immediately regret letting my imagination wander.

"And then Lessie fucking Marcela happened." Elsa gazes at her clasped hands. Her mouth moves a few times before any words come out. "Ethan was building up his business. After his parents got set up, we took a big hit, but Ethan wanted to build things back like before."

"Better than before," Gabriel adds.

"Sure. And he did good. It didn't take long for people to realize he would be *the* gun runner in Mountain City."

"Everything was going great," Gabriel says. "Until Lessie Marcela showed up, some done-up Mage cunt in a giant SUV that rolled around like she owned the world."

That would be the woman I took the pictures of. The one Burgess hired me to photograph. Suddenly, I don't know that I want to hear any more of the story.

Elsa holds the jar of Deer Piss but doesn't drink. "Lessie told Ethan he was going to run guns to Downtown for her. Ethan takes a lot of things, but one thing he does not take is orders."

Gabriel laughs. "He told that bitch to get lost."

"But she didn't?" I have a crushing feeling I know how this story ends. I swallow the lump in my throat, or my pride, whatever.

"No." Elsa traces her finger around the rim of the jar. The jar hums a warbling, dissonant note. "Lessie told Ethan she would kill the ones he loved. Ethan tried to get Fox into hiding, but you know her."

I do know her. No way in hell anyone could ever threaten her away. "Yeah."

Gabriel clears his throat. "The threats got more intense, more direct. Packages of dead foxes came in the mail. Lessie dropped by wearing fox furs. Fox wouldn't leave though. Nothing scares that stubborn woman." Gabriel pounds his fist against the tailgate.

Was Burgess behind all of this? Did he hire Lessie to run the guns and then hire me to catch her? That's one hell of a way to ruin the Hair's reputation. It's neat though. Lessie mysterious got shanked in prison and word *somehow* leaked out that I was the one who took the pictures, practically ensuring Ethan would take retribution.

"One night, a Mage snuck into the compound. Must have got by with cloaking of some sort." Elsa sighs. "The Mage attacked Ethan and Fox in their bed. Ethan killed the Mage, but not before…" Elsa turns away.

Gabriel slides off the truck. He moves around to take Elsa in his arms. "The Mage cut Fox up bad. She bled out in Ethan's arms. That's the last we'd heard of her until tonight."

"Holy shit." Jordon crouches in the truck bed behind me. His eyes are wide as fists. "How did she survive?"

The Hairs turn to me.

I hold my hands up. "Don't look at me, first I've heard this story."

"Oh, come on, man." Jordon sits next to me. "You telling me your wife never told you about her near death experience?"

"We made a deal never to ask about each other's past."

"No way. I don't buy it," Gabriel says.

I hold up two fingers. "Scout's honor. How else could two old folks like us be married without turning into jealous monsters over our pasts?"

The trio of wolves break out in laughter.

"What?" I don't get it.

"It's just that you looked real not jealous over Ethan back there," Elsa says, wiping a tear out of the corner of her eye.

I sigh. "I need a cigarette."

Jordon is all too quick to hand me a smoke. Probably happy that he's old enough to do something with the group. Either way, I accept his offering, and the other two wolves help themselves to the kid's sticks.

We smoke in silence for a few minutes. Just me and three of my closest canine friends out for a quick buzz out under the moonlight. These guys aren't so bad when they're not trying to kill me.

The alcohol warms my insides, and the nicotine puts my nerves on ice for the moment. "So what's it like, for you guys? I mean now that everything's all fucked up?" Must be working on my brain, too. There's no way I should have said that.

"Now that you fucked it up, you mean?" There's a hint of danger in Gabriel's voice, but not the outright threat of his Alpha from earlier.

"Yeah, I guess."

"Imagine everyone hating you," Elsa says.

"Before they even meet you, or know you." Jordon coughs as he exhales a small cloud.

"No one gives a single damn what you've done, or who you are. You've automatically done something wrong, just for being a Hair." Gabriel clicks his tongue as he flicks his cigarette out of the truck and into the grass.

"You ever read about the Purging?" Elsa asks.

"Read about it? I was alive for it."

The truck shifts as the wolves move for a better look at me. The Purging happened over a hundred years back. Humans found out about Mages and went on a witch hunt. It was a big deal down south. Everyone hears about the bullshit that went on in Salem, but here, in Mountain City, the tales never escaped these hills. The Purging made Salem look like a couple bored housewives trying to stir up some excitement. The steets of Mountain City ran red with blood. Guilty blood. Innocent blood. Just, blood.

"Right. Well, at least those Mages could act human and hope they didn't get caught. We look different. People can pick us out. And they do. They point and throw things and yell." Elsa isn't looking at me anymore. Her gaze is off in the stars somewhere.

Gabriel takes her hand in his, nuzzles the back of her hand against his cheek. "Things aren't as bad as the Purging yet, but Burgess is determined to make every single resident in Mountain City hate us. That old man keeps pouring gas on this thing and it's just one spark away from the flame of war."

"Elsa, Gabriel, Jordon, I'm sorry. For everything. I didn't know it would lead to this."

Hinges screech as the door to the warehouse swings open. I take one running lunge of a step before I catch myself. I try to play it off cool and stroll over to Fox and a smiling Ethan.

"Did everyone play nice?" Fox adjusts a large black duffle bag slung over her shoulder.

"Yeah. We had a real interesting talk."

Fox gives me an odd glance. I don't think my words were slurred, were they?

"Did they...?" Fox's gaze jumps to Gabriel and Elsa.

"Sure did." Gabriel smiles anxiously, slaps me on the back.

Fox opens the door of the Mustang and leans the seat forward. She slips the bag inside. Metal clangs against metal. "Have a good night, Ethan." Fox drops into the driver seat. "You, too, Gabriel, Elsa," she says through the open window.

Gabriel's cheeks redden. Elsa flashes a quick grin at Fox.

"And you, new kid." She blows Jordon a kiss, and the kid swoons.

I've never seen a two hundred fifty pound werewolf swoon until right this moment. I get in the car.

Ethan sets his hands on Fox's door, leans his head in the car. "Be safe out there, Orange Coat."

145

"You know me," Fox says with a devilish grin. My devilish grin. That smile is for *me only*, goddammit.

"Yes, I do know you. Here, take this." Ethan takes a remote the size of a car clicker out of his pocket and hands it to Fox. There's one red button in the middle of it with the outline of a howling wolf in black. "If you get in over your head, or you need me for any reason, press that button."

Fox holds the clicker up to the light coming from floods around the building. "What is this?"

"I worked out a deal with a couple Mages who were looking for some automatics. There are only two right now." Ethan takes a matching one out of his pocket. "But soon, my entire pack will carry one. You remember Slim McGinley?"

"Yeah." Fox laughs. "That kid couldn't hold whiskey to save his life. That one Christmas he got slushed on Deer Piss and sprayed everyone he saw with a fire extinguisher."

Ethan gives a sad smile. "A couple weeks back a few redneck Standards got drunk. They jumped Slim Downtown, tied him to the hitch of their truck, and drug him all the way back to my doorstep."

"Oh," Fox says, her hands curl into balls, "fuck. Is he…?"

Ethan shakes his head, turns back toward the building for a few beats. "None of my pack will get caught like that again. That's why I'm having these made. Anyway, if you press that button, a red wolf will light up the sky above you. Even if we are indoors, the entire pack will see it. We will come to help."

Fox nods at Ethan's pocket. "Only two, and you have the other one?"

"I tried to give it to Elsa, but they made me keep it. As Alpha, they are worried someone will attack me first. I can take care of myself, I told them that, but…"

"But even the pack can out rule the Alpha if they try hard enough. I remember how things work."

"I'm sure you do." Ethan flashes a toothy grin, canines sparkling in the moonlight. Even with his eyes welled up with emotion, the gesture carries its intended meaning.

I want to reach across the car and knock his teeth down his throat.

As if she can read me, Fox lays her hand on mine. She turns the wedding ring around my finger. "Thanks, Ethan, for everything, but I think Sam and I have to get going."

"You sure you don't need me to come with you?" Ethan practically has the door opened to hop in the back seat.

"No, we're good."

The Hair takes his hand off the door and leans his head in, giving me a predatory stare. "If you get her hurt, I swear I will murder you and you won't come back. Understand me?" Ethan's eyes flash yellow.

"Loud and clear, captain." I salute. *What, get her killed like you did?* The comeback echoes in my mind, but I can't bring myself to say it.

Ethan's face is red, his eyes bloodshot. I try to imagine losing Fox. Then I try to imagine her coming back from the dead—and marrying someone else? Yeah, Ethan's had enough comebacks for one night.

The engine revs, and we take off down the road, unharmed and well-armed.

Chapter 15

Fox aims the car southwest toward Downtown, but at a much slower pace. "So, I guess we need to figure out a plan."

"Honey," I take her hand, "I know I promised never to ask you about your past, and you don't have to tell me, but what happened with Ethan?"

"What did Gabriel and Elsa tell you?"

"They told me about Lessie and that a Mage broke in and killed you."

"It wasn't one Mage. There were two. They both had some form of invisibility spell. The first cut woke me up. I fought and clawed at the attacker. When I injured the Mage, he became visible. Maybe he couldn't concentrate on the spell. I don't know. Ethan tackled the guy he could see, but the second attacker cut me more. I knew I wasn't going to live in that body, so I grabbed hold of the Mage. My soul moved to the invisible Mage, and I split, leaving my old body to die."

"Why not tell Ethan? Why go off the grid?"

"Two reasons. First, Ethan is stubborn. If he didn't lose, he'd keep fighting the Mages or whoever and eventually they would kill someone for real. Maybe me, or Gabriel, or Ethan, or Elsa, or anyone else. It didn't matter. I knew if Ethan lost me, it would break him, and he would agree to the deal to stop the bloodshed. Ethan's a tough bastard, but he will do anything to keep his pack out of harm's way."

Fox holds the wheel with her knees and touches the back of her hand to her eye. The fingers of her other hand squeeze tight against mine.

"What's the second reason?"

"Ethan is persistent. He kept proposing, and I kept putting him off. I loved Ethan, but I just wasn't ready to commit my life to him. And I'm sure you've heard, breaking up with a Hair is pretty hard to do. The attack was my out. A clean slate. The safest possible exit for me and for Ethan."

I drum on my thigh. I open the glove box, close it. Roll the window down a crack. Drum my fingers more. "You still love him?"

Fox turns directly to me, her eyes fixed on mine. "I love you, Samuel Flint. That's why I married you and not Ethan. That's why I asked you to marry me."

"Oh."

Feel better now, stupid?

That damn voice in my head is going to drive me crazy.

"Now stop with the jealous spouse thing." Fox slaps my thigh. "You're bad at it."

"So why go back now?"

"Because we need firepower, and Ethan is hands-down the best arms dealer in Mountain City. That, and he takes our credit."

"Good point." I want to argue for argument's sake, but there's no real reason for it.

I reach into the back seat for the duffel bag. The thing weighs a ton. With the bag unzipped, a small armory reveals itself.

"Fuck." I grab my pistol. "I forgot to get my bullets back from that Hair kid Jordon."

"Do three bullets really mean that much with a battalion's worth of guns in your lap?"

"No, but I really like this gun."

Necrotown: Mountain City Chronicles

"Here." Fox clicks on the dome light and reaches into the bag. "I picked one up just for you." Fox hands me the biggest six-shooter I've ever seen.

I hold the gun up to the window. Daylight is just breaking over the mountains. The orange glow shines in my eyes, and I blink back tears as the light sets off a massive migraine I didn't know I had. I tilt my head away from the sun and examine the hand cannon. The antique barrel is the size of my forearm and carved with runes I don't recognize. I flick the cylinder open. Each bullet is the size of a prescription pill bottle.

"Holy hell, Fox, this thing'll blow my arm off if I try to shoot it."

"No, no." Fox takes the Downtown exit. "That's what the markings are for. Ethan said one is for recoil, one is for accuracy, and one is for…um, I don't remember, but it should be awesome."

"Where do I get bullets for this monster?" I close the cylinder, check to make sure the safety is on. Probably blow a hole through the floorboard if this thing accidentally fired. That and the highway, and everything between here and China, as a matter of fact.

"About that. Ethan only had six bullets, and they are all in the gun. So, shoot wisely."

I sight passing signs with the gun, debate about popping a shot off at a 'Lloyd F. Burgess Sponsored Bridge' plaque-type thing, but it's not worth the wasted ammo. Between Burgess and Sarah, I'm going to need a couple dozen of these bullets.

Fox parks us in a garage below Burgess's building. We take an elevator to the lobby. The entire first floor of the building is decked out in glass and chrome.

Driving by at the wrong time of day is a nightmare. There are enough traffic accidents from the bottom floor glare alone that some citizens petitioned to have something done. But, Lloyd owns city hall, in a metaphorical sense anyway. The petition got denied.

The front desk clerk has all the charm of a haunted house door-knocker with none of the brass. The guy's name is probably Tucker. Or Declan. Or Ethan. Yeah, screw guys named Ethan.

"Excuse me, sir," I say in my most cordial voice.

The guy holds up a finger for me to wait. He's not on the phone. He's not typing on the computer. Hell, he's not even playing with his personal phone. There is not one single damn reason for him to tell me to wait.

I'm about to slap the desk to get his attention—better the desk than his face, right?—when he swivels in his chair and turns his Ken-doll grin on me. His name tag reads: Oliver. That sounds right. Oliver tugs at the corners of his bow tie. "May I *help* you?" The help would have come through gritted teeth if Oliver had enough muscle in his delicate features to do that sort of thing.

"We're here to see Lloyd Burgess," I say.

"Start with an appointment. Mr. Burgess doesn't usually take," Oliver pauses to look Fox and I over, "homeless people in without an appointment."

"Burgess hired me to work for him. He'll want to hear what I've got say. So go back to slicking your hair while I go talk to boss man."

Oliver slides his sleeves up. It might be intimidating if his forearms weren't the size of healthy toothpicks. "No. I'm not even giving you access to Mr. Burgess's level until his secretary calls down here and tells me to send you in."

I smile at Oliver. The affection is so sincere my jaw pops. I rest my forearms against the cool steel of the counter and lean in close. "Hey, guy," I say in a quiet-ish voice, "I'm a private investigator. And the job Lloyd hired me for is a little...sensitive." I raise my voice to just below a shout and say, "So unless you want me telling everyone about the hooker-fueled weekend in Vegas he claims not to remember..."

Oliver freaks the shit out. His face turns seven shades of red, and he fans his arms through the air to get me to hush. "Sh-shhh-just-shh." His gaze darts around the lobby to anyone who might be watching us. The desk clerk is too panicked to realize no one gives a fuck if it's not happening on their cell phone. I could do more damage with a status update than I could screaming bloody murder.

"Well?" I say.

"Just, just go get in the damn elevator." There's a vein in Oliver's forehead big enough to drink a milkshake through.

Fox and I head through the sliding doors for our ride up to that deluxe office in the sky. We don't even have to press a button. Once the doors close, the elevator automatically starts up for the top floor. I'm guessing Oliver controls that.

After a seventeen-minute ride to the stratosphere, the elevator 'bings' and the doors open. Two armed guards stand to either side. The fact that they are armed is so pointless I have to swallow to keep from laughing. They are Mages, and each one is vacuuming enough power out of the air to pull a rabbit out of a black hole while sawing a woman in half while submerged in a tank of piranhas. Needless to say, these guys are running enough current to take care of just about any threat without the need of automatics tucked under their arms.

"Easy boys," I say, glad we left our weapons in the car. "We're just here to talk to the boss."

"It's okay, boys, let them through," a woman says from behind the magical tag team.

Silently, the two men step to the side, allowing a full view of Burgess's empire. The entire floor must serve as Bugess' office, but just outside the elevator is a small lobby, small as compared to the Atlantic Ocean anyway. The place is enough to make Midas sick. Gold floors, gold walls, a solid gold desk for the secretary, a gold statue of George Washington—or maybe that's Papa Burgess, I dunno—even a solid gold fucking palm tree. As if gold or palm trees are native to Mountain City.

We approach the desk, and I'm thankful there aren't windows on the interior because the thing is polished enough to shatter glass with glare if full light ever hit it.

"Mr. and Mrs. Flint, I assume?" The woman sitting behind the desk in a golden office chair—get this, even the fabric on the chair looks like it was woven in gold—stares at us appraisingly.

The secretary is a couple months over twenty and a couple buttons short of chaste. She's got dark hair, pale skin, and soft green eyes, and I swear I've seen her before. I glance over and Fox is staring at the woman with a curled lip. Maybe Fox recognizes her from somewhere?

"Yeah, that's us. Could we have a word with good ol' Lloyd?" My hands starts to smack the desk for inflection, but I get a glimpse of the million-dollar finish and decide I should probably keep my grubby mitts off of it.

The secretary snarls. "Mr. Burgess is expecting you." She looks down and fastens the top couple buttons of her blouse like she's just now realized she's as desperate for attention as the rest of this place.

"Trust me, kid, I'm not looking." I walk to the only other door.

"Fuckin' better not be," Fox whispers behind me. "You're old enough to be her great, great, blah, blah, great grandfather."

"You're the only one for me, love," I say. I, for one, have never understood the obsession with scantily clad teenagers. They all look like children. Fox is a woman—or at least possessing the body of a woman—and *that* is a beautiful thing.

The interior of Burgess's office isn't any less over-indulgent. His office takes up one entire half of the floor, wall to wall. The other

153

half is sectioned off behind partitions, private quarters of some sort if I had to guess. The room is as gold as the lobby, but the desk and chair are some really old looking wood. Oak, maybe?

Two more armed guards flank Burgess. I take a deep breath and close my eyes. The room smells woody from the desk, but beyond that I feel for the magic. The two Mages are drawing so hard I can't even taste a hint of the power in the air. They are prepped for war. Too prepped for one incompetent Quasi-Immortal and a Kitsune. What kind of company is Burgess expecting?

"You don't have Sarah," Burgess says. His voice is darker than the liver spots on his half-bald head.

"We seem to have been sent into some shit that was over our pay grades. What the hell is Sarah's deal?" I ask. Anger spikes in my chest; I wasn't *that* angry until I said it out loud.

Burgess leans back in his chair. The chair doesn't squeak. Rich fucks get all the comforts in life. "Sarah is scared. She needs to come back so I can help her through this."

"Help her through what, exactly?" Fox steps forward, plants her fists on Burgess's desk.

"As I'm sure you noticed, Sarah has special...abilities. She needs me to coach her, to help her."

"Special abilities?" I should have brought my gun. "She can control the dead. That goes so far beyond *special abilities* I don't even know where to start."

"All the more reason you need to find her, and bring her back." Burgess steeples his fingers and tries to look tough, but there's a tick at the corner of his eye. Is he afraid? "I will pay any price."

I open my mouth to bring up my parents, but before I can get a word out Fox's voice cuts across the room.

"She doesn't want to come back," Fox says.

"Naïve rebels never do want to come home, do they, Mrs. Flint?"

"Tell me why she doesn't want to come back to you, Lloyd?" Fox's knuckles are practically burrowing holes in the desk.

"She's a stupid girl. Just do what I'm paying you for and bring her home."

"Why, so you can fuck your daughter more?" The rage in Fox's voice could melt half the gold in the room.

I'm slightly confused.

Burgess kicks the chair back as he stands and plants his hands on the desk opposite Fox. His face burns red. "She's not my—" Burgess stops in his tracks. He takes a deep breath.

"Not what? Not your fuck toy?" Fox's face matches the red tint of her hair. I don't know that I've ever seen her like this. "Don't give me that bullshit. Are you going to sit here and tell me it's just a coincidence your bimbo of a secretary looks identical to your daughter?"

Oh, shit. That's why she looks so familiar. Fox is right. The secretary looks just like Sarah.

"I won't deny it."

"And you're sleeping with your secretary."

"Yes." Burgess answers, stone cold. His honesty is a little surprising.

"You're fucking your secretary who looks like a copy of your daughter. And now you are desperate to find that very same daughter who wants nothing to do with you. Keep your incestual, pedophiliac money to yourself. We are done." Fox turns for the door, and I'm a half step behind her.

Necrotown: Mountain City Chronicles

The vacuum of power in the air explodes outward toward us. My throat closes, and my feet become lead weights. Energy spins me around to face Burgess again. Fox is frozen next to me, gasping for air that won't come. Neither of the Mages break a sweat. Those guys are pros.

I try to swallow, but my throat won't work. It's frozen closed. My lungs burn in my chest as they fight to pump air through a sealed hatch. Out of the corner of my eye I spot Fox shaking, turning purple. I try to close my eyes, to focus on the power the Mages are using. Maybe I can undo it. The magic is strong, it tastes like coffee and sweat.

Using the little knowledge I have, I rip at the tendrils of energy with my mind. My old Mage of a mentor always told me my problem was that I couldn't commit. Time and time again, he told me the only thing that kept me from being a half-decent Mage was myself. I try to let it all go and fight the magic.

Fingers snap and the hold on my throat loosens. I suck in a gasp of air, and it's the most glorious thing I've ever felt. My muscles give up, and I collapse forward. The energy catches me, pushes me back up to my feet, and holds me there.

Burgess stands in front of me. I'm not sure how he got there or how long he's been there. All I'm concerned with is that I can breathe. Fox is breathing again, too.

"Now that I have your attention, listen to me." Burgess leans in close to Fox—on her knees where the Mage released her—his forehead pressed against the top of her head. "*Both* of you. You've got me wrong. You think you are smart, but you aren't."

Burgess takes a seat at his desk. "Complete this job, and I will pay you beyond your wildest dream. Walk away, and I won't stop until I see you both dead. Permanently."

Burgess waves a hand, and the two Mages toss us out into the lobby like a failed stage act.

Chapter 16

"What the hell was that about?" I slam my car door shut. The two Mages have followed us all the way from Burgess' office.

"What do you mean 'What was that all about'? The dirty old man is sleeping with his daughter. Or if he's not, he wants to. His secretary looked like a carbon copy of Sarah, but a year or two older." Fox gives each of the Mages their own special wave.

It's a good thing we locked the weapons in the trunk. I wouldn't put it past her to take potshots at them as we drive away. I start the car and ease out of the parking space, trying not to make any more of a scene than we've already made. Oliver seemed quite pleased with our heavily-armed escort from the building.

Fox lowers her window. "Fuck you very much," she shouts at the Mages as we drive by. So much for discrete. Then again, yeah, fuck those guys.

"Maybe Sarah looks like her mother, and Burgess hired the secretary because she looks like the late Mrs. Burgess?" The argument sounds weak, even to me.

"Yeah, that's likely." If the sarcasm were anything thicker, it would get caught in her throat. "We need to blow town. Forget Sarah, forget Burgess, forget this whole fucked-up city."

"We can't leave." I point the car in no particular direction other than 'away from Lloyd Burgess' and turn onto the main road through Downtown.

"Why? You hate Mountain City and the Glow especially." Fox props her sneakered feet up on the dash and digs a cigarette out of her jeans. The soft, green pack is crumpled from being shoved into her small pockets, and the cigarette she pulls out has a crease in the middle of it. She lights it, doesn't offer me one.

"Did you hear Burgess back there? If we split, he'll come for us, and he happens to be the *one* guy in Mountain City rich enough to make our lives hell."

"We are both pretty resourceful. I think we'll make it." Fox's feet bounce on the dash as she takes a puff and blows the smoke out the window.

A bloody, cut-up Fox appears in my mind, dying in Ethan's arms. That won't happen to me. "I'm not taking the chance. I can't risk losing you. I love you too much."

"Awww, that's sweet. But I'm not risking my life to kidnap the most powerful Necromancer in existence and take her back to her pedophile of a father."

She's got a good point. I reach over and snatch the cigarette from her hand. There's only one drag left, but I take it. Sarah is terrifying. Could Burgess really be sleeping with his daughter? The family is demented, but is it that demented?

"You remember when you accused Burgess of sleeping with his daughter? What was his first response?"

Fox chews on her lip for a moment while she grabs a crumpled pair of cigarettes from her pocket. She throws the empty pack into the back seat with about seven dozen others. "He said she's not my lover or something."

"No. He said, 'She's not my,' and stopped. His whole demeanor changed like he almost slipped up and said some shit he wasn't supposed to."

"Okay, Sarah's not his what?" Fox hands me a smoke.

"I don't know, but there's a guy who might." The Mountain City jailhouse is the last place I feel like going, but the universe doesn't seem to give much of a damn about what I want.

"Who?"

"It's best if you meet him in person."

The jailhouse isn't far. We are there in a couple minutes. I wish I could take a drink before we go in, but the whiskey is back home. No time. The sooner we figure this out, the better. We go in, we get answers, we fix this mess, and we break for the beach, first chance.

There is a parking garage across the street, and I find the darkest, quietest corner. "Okay, honey, get in the back seat and lay down. I'm going to need you to hitch a ride inside and we need to keep your body out of sight for a bit." I put my hand on Fox's.

She climbs into the back and stretches out on the floorboard, on top of all the cigarette packs. "Are we about to break in to prison?" Fox asks with a grin. Only my wife would be excited about sneaking into jail.

"Actually, my dear, we are about to break someone out." I glance back at her curled up on the floor.

Fox's whole body tenses with excitement. She'd be jumping up and down if there were room for that sort of thing. She grabs my arm, and Sune crosses over onto my hand. The fox takes residence on my forearm and winks at me.

This isn't the first time Sune has been on me, but it's rare. I'm still in complete control of my thoughts and body, but I can feel Fox at the edges of my being. I treasure the closeness I share with my wife, but this particular kind of closeness isn't my favorite. This is with me in complete control, I can't imagine what it's like when Fox actually takes over someone's body. Let's hope I never find out.

I lock the car and walk across the street.

The inside of the jail is somewhat crowded. There are three guards working behind the desk, a Hair is sitting with handcuffs, leg shackles, and a new brand still smoking on the side of his neck. A young guy with his collar popped sits next to the Hair, unfettered.

159

"Ey, this some ol' bowl ship," the young guy spews. A fifth of vodka soaks his breath.

"Shut yer damn mouth," the Hair says.

"Fuhck y-you, hairball." The guy's chest swells up, pushing his pink popped-collar up to his ears. The lion or dog or whatever the hell stitched into the breast of his shirt looks like it's about to tear in half.

"Kid, your Stone dumb ass will be out of here soon enough. If I'm going to be stuck here, I'd rather be stuck in silence."

The Stone shakes, angry. He rears a club-sized fist back and takes his shot. The Hair catches the Stone's fist in his hand.

"Hey," one guard shouts, "the Hair is attacking that kid."

The three guards rush around the counter, electric batons in hand. One guard shoves the Stone out of the way. The guy stumbles over a bench and hits the ground in a drunken stupor. The three guards work on the Hair with their buzzers.

The werewolf's eyes blaze yellow, but that's as close as he can get to his inner beast with the brand on his neck. Inside I can feel Fox's conscious pacing. Her hatred for these cops and her need to rip them to pieces is burning in my chest and itching at the back of my brain.

"Easy, killer," I say under my breath. "This isn't our fight, not right now."

Do something. Fox's voice echoes in my mind. She sounds hurt.

I clear my throat, loud. "Excuse me, gentlemen?" The three guards turn on me.

The Hair is unconscious, slumped over against his restraints.

"I have a client to meet with and time is of the essence, so if you wouldn't mind..." I tap my wrist for the watch I'm not wearing.

"Yeah, sure," one guard says. He walks back to his station.

"Hey, kid," a tall, skinny guard says to the drunken Stone on the floor. "I guess getting brutalized by one of them animals is punishment enough. You learned your lesson?"

The Stone stares, glaze-eyed at the lights in the ceiling.

"I'd take that for a yes. Why don't you be on your way?" The guard nods to the door.

"How can I help you?" The guard in front of us speaks with the impatient tone of a guy who hates his job.

"I'm here to see a client," I say.

"Done said that," guard says. "Which client?"

"Old man downstairs. Mage. White hair. A bit crazy."

The guard laughs. "I thought you said it was urgent. That old-timer has been down there half a century."

"Recent break in his case. Can I see him now?"

"Sure, just let me get prints."

"Perfect," I say.

The guard grabs a print sheet. "Here." He tosses it on the counter. Apparently he's not going to help. I take my right middle finger and print it where my left thumb should go.

"Really?" The guard grabs my hand and forces my finger to the right spot.

Sune moves down my forearm and onto the guard. There are all kinds of wards to prevent magic in jails, but Fox is a rare breed and what she does isn't exactly magic. The jail has nothing to stop her, and the transformation is instant. GuardFox winks at me, and I finish my prints without incident.

"Say, fellas," GuardFox says, "I'm going to take this guy to the cell so he doesn't get any funny ideas."

"Good thinking," the tall guard says. "Especially since it's protocol."

"Yeah, right," GuardFox says. "Come on, let's go."

GuardFox leads me back to the cell she picked me up from the other day. "So why exactly are we back here?"

"I made a friend, of sorts."

"You don't have any friends, Sam."

"Touché, but I do have a sexy-ass wife."

GuardFox slaps my ass. That is exactly as awkward as it sounds. I look back with a cocked eyebrow. "Sorry," she says. "Habit."

I walk down to the cell where I met the old man a couple days ago. "Psst, you still in there?"

The old man steps out of the shadows, ear-to-ear smile. "Come back for answers, Sammy-boy?"

"Something like that," I say.

"Information isn't free." The man steps back and holds his arms out.

"Fox, let the guy out."

GuardFox grabs a key off her belt and unlocks the door. For all the technology in the world, the safest form of jailing is still old-fashioned, mechanical locks made with iron parts.

"There," I say. "Spill it, what do you know about Burgess?"

The man walks out of his cell and stands to his full height, his spine cracks with a series of pops. He isn't tall by any means, but freedom has added a couple inches.

"It's not safe to talk here," the man says. "What if the other guards see?" He eyes GuardFox with a strange kind of interest.

"You really think these assholes give two shits about security cameras? That one light doesn't even shine down the entire hall." GuardFox points at the one, pathetic light source.

"Even still, I could use some fresh air. Would you mind?"

GuardFox glances over her shoulder. "Fine. Just follow me and act like a prisoner if we come across anyone. All right, old man?"

"Name is Bartholomew Gorstein. And, yes, I can manage."

We head back up the stairs and onto the main level. Instead of turning out toward the lobby, we go a different direction. Fox is probably counting on a back entrance.

Her intuition is right. There's an emergency exit at the back. GuardFox puts a hand on the bar to open the door.

"Wait," I say, "what about the alarm?"

Bartholomew steps up. He extends a finger and a lightning strike of energy shoots to the alarm control box. "Taken care of."

GuardFox tentatively pushes the lever, and the door silently opens.

Mental note: Be wary of the Mage who's been locked up for half a century.

"There's a café across the street," GuardFox says. "You two go there, and I'll meet up with you."

163

"Wait. Where are you going?"

"I've got to get back to keep from arousing suspicions. I'll hop back in my ride and meet you guys over there."

"Wait, how are you going to get back in your body when—"

GuardFox pushes Bartholomew and me out the door and slams it shut. Being a fire exit, there's no handle outside. Looks like my new friend and I are heading for the café.

Bartholomew whistles. "She's something."

"Sure is. Anything you can do about that?" I point at the Mage's raggedy prison-issue outfit.

The Mage closes his eyes and takes a deep breath. A swell of energy sweeps in his direction. He snaps his fingers, and he's a new person. His hair is cut and slicked back, beard trimmed to a manageable pair of chops, and clothing swapped for something worthy of a black tie affair.

"Not bad," I say. This guy's got some juice.

"Thank you." Bartholomew holds the edges of his vest. His left eye twitches three times.

He's got his shit as together as any of the rest of us, I suppose.

Chapter 17

Bartholomew and I take a seat at a table with four chairs. I order two black coffees.

"Okay, what do you know?"

"Take it easy. Let's wait on your little fox to come back, yeah?" The Mage sips his coffee and moans like he's never tasted Mooncents coffee.

"Fox?" How does he know that?

"I'm not psychic, but I saw the tattoo. Kitsune wasn't a far leap."

"That's a pretty good spot," I say. "Most people wouldn't guess Kitsune even with the tattoo dancing in front of their eyes."

"I'm not most people," Bartholomew says.

That is becoming very apparent.

Our coffees are down to dregs by the time Fox hurries to our table with the black duffel bag from the car slung over her shoulder. I stand up and pull a chair out for her. "Are you okay? How did you get back?"

Fox slides the black bag under the table and takes a seat. "I'm fine. Don't worry about me." She sweeps a lock of hair behind her ear. There's a red smear across her neck.

"Jesus, Fox, is that blood?" I grab a napkin, dip it in a cup of water on our table, and wipe at the mark.

"Oh, shit. It's nothing." She takes the napkin and finishes cleaning.

Our waitress comes up to the table. "Can I get you anything else?"

The Mage smiles up at the waitress. Being out of his cage seems to have given him confidence, and this is probably the first woman he's seen in quite some time. There's a hunger in his smile that makes me wonder if I'm about to have to put a rabid dog down. "A refill would be exquisite, darling."

The waitress blushes, and her gaze flicks to me.

"Do you have whiskey?" I ask.

"Christ," she says, "it's hardly even afternoon."

"Just asking." Down in the Glow, you have to ask to not have a splash of amber anti-depressant in your coffee. Apparently these folks Downtown do not feel the same. "I'll just have a refill also."

"I'd like the biggest size, strongest coffee you have," Fox says. She crumples the napkin up so that most of the red is out of view.

The waitress whirls away with a sweep of her green apron, Birkenstock shoes squeaking across the faded linoleum with every step.

"Well," Bartholomew says, "I should have thought to ask for a little pick me up. You think it's too late to ask her to add something a little stiff to mine?" He stares in her direction. "Or maybe I can add a little something stiff—"

Fox slams a knife down—it could have come from anywhere, tucked under clothing, tied up in her hair; Fox is never unarmed—into the table in front of the Mage. The knife buries itself to the hilt directly over Bartholomew's lap. His left eye twitches a half dozen times.

"Not another fucking word unless it's about Sam and/or those rich pricks on the hill." She unsticks the knife from the table and sets it in her lap, in plain view of anyone looking.

"Start at the beginning," I say.

The Mage gives a patient smile. He has to have known this was coming. "My name is Bartholomew Gorstein, and I am, was, quite the powerful magic-wrangler in my day. People came from all over to watch me work. One day, this man approached me with a job. He said he had more money than I could ever dream of."

"That would be Burgess?" I ask.

"Yes. Mr. Burgess offered me a check with more zeroes than I thought possible—to oversee a ceremony. Once he told me who he was, I recognized him—knew he was good for the money he offered. So I said, sure, I would oversee his ceremony. Others had asked the same of me. Little things like love spells or make-my-kid-the-next-Mozart spells or the like. Bullshit that hardly ever worked worth a damn, but people always wanted to believe."

The waitress brings the drinks and sets them in front of us. Bartholomew opens his mouth to say something, but at the last minute he glances at Fox and seems to change his mind. Some women control with their feminine wiles; Fox does just fine with her feminine fuck-with-me-and-I-will-castrate-you-ness. That's sexy as hell.

"Mr. Burgess didn't tell me where we were meeting. On the day of the job, a chauffeur picked me up in a stretch Rolls Royce. He drove me to Necrotown."

"That didn't make you nervous?" I swirl the last of my empty coffee in the cup. Grounds whirl around with the last splash of liquid.

"Maybe other people, but the Necros never scared me. Their graveyard magic is little more than chicken bones and Tarot cards. Or at least that's what I thought of it until I met Burgess."

167

My chest tightens. There is no way I'm going to like what's coming.

"I can stop if this story makes you uncomfortable, Mr. Flint."

"Keep going." I force the words past a locked jaw.

"Of all the things I've seen in my long life, before and after, I've never seen anything like that night. This woman, Burgess's wife Sandra, lay on a stretcher over a pit of green fire. She just floated there, as if suspended by the flames. Above her, a man and a woman hung upside down, ankles shackled to the ceiling, arms behind their backs."

My fist clenches. I look down to find a fork I didn't know I was holding bent like a paperclip. My heart beats faster and faster until it feels like it's going to stop at any second. Back at the jail, the Mage said this had to do with my parents. Those aren't my parents, those aren't my parents. Those aren't my parents.

I don't want to hear another word.

I can't stand another word.

I have to know.

"Yes, the couple hanging from the ceiling were Quasi-Immortals by the name of Flint."

Fox sucks in a gasp. Her hand is on top of mine in an instant. The warmth is the only comfort as the blood drains from my body. Burgess killed my parents?

The waitress brings us three coffees. I think. I don't remember seeing her, but I'm drinking boiling hot coffee. The drink burns my tongue and the roof of my mouth. When I set the cup back down, it shakes against the top of the table.

"As it turns out, Burgess's wife was dying. He did everything he could to save the woman. Healers and mystics and Mages and

Herbalistas and the rest. They all failed. To this day, I have no idea where he found it but he found it but he found a spell for eternal life."

"And you were just the sap he needed to perform it?" Fox sits perfectly still, rapt in the story.

"I was. Magic, like life, is tricky. There are all these checks and balances. Some call it God, others Nature. Others still don't know what to call it, but they respect it. Nature has a way. To give life, life needs taken. To give eternal life, eternal life needs taken. Not just one, but two. Two Quasi-Immortal sacrifices, carved with runes so ancient I'd never glimpsed them before."

"Carved?" The word comes out raspy. I almost choke on it.

"Yes, carved." Bartholomew takes a drink from his coffee, calm as if he were telling campfire stories. "Carved with a knife burning with the flames of the damned. Green fire, if you didn't guess. It couldn't have been something easy, a circle or a pentagram. No, it had to be these complex concentric dots and lines, from head to toe."

Sweat rolls down my forehead. I blink and a drop drips into my eye. The salt burns. The tears welling up are from the burn. They aren't from hurt. Or anger. When I get my hands on Burgess, he's going to wish that he had just been sleeping with his daughter. I'm going to rip that rich prick to shreds. I touch the back of my wrist to the corners of my eyes.

All the years not knowing where my parents went, and it was because of some greedy fucking Standard.

Bartholomew appraises me with his gaze for a few moments before he sighs and continues. "Anyway, I guess you don't need all the details. You're looking a little green there, pal."

"What happened next?" I try to keep my voice calm, collected; I fail.

"If you insist." Bartholomew shrugs. "I made the carvings on their skin and did the incantations. The magic was incredible, power I've never felt before. Eventually, they both bleed out from the cuts. The next part of the spell allowed me to capture their souls so they couldn't return to their home for reanimation."

I rotate my head in a circle. A loud pop echoes from my spine. "Are you telling me you prevented their reincarnation?" I slide my hand out from Fox's grip and close it on the hilt of the knife in her lap.

"Exactly, I wouldn't have thought it possible either, but this stuff Burgess dug up was some real heavy duty magic."

"Go on, what happened next?" The metal handle of Fox's knife is cold against my palm. There is nothing warm about death.

Fox slides a hand on top of my thigh.

"I formed the two souls into this ball of… pure energy. Pure magical energy unlike anything I've ever felt. It tasted clean, almost soapy, but in a refreshing way. Something like a new-life-smell, you know? Well, I guess not."

"Get the fuck on with it," I say. My racing heartbeat pulses against the back of my eyes, blurring my vision with every pump. I need him to finish the story so I have all the information. Then I can kill him.

"Burgess's wife, she was dying of uterine cancer or something like that. He instructed me to bond the energy with her there. I did as he said, but something didn't take. She died there on the table." Bartholomew's eye twitches a handful of times. He sips his coffee.

"Where does Sarah Roswell come into all of this?" Fox asks.

Bartholomew smiles. He's putting on a show. "After Sandra died, her body started decomposing. Almost instantly she faded to nothing like a thousand years passed in a blink. Skin shriveled, rotted, disappeared to nothing but bone, but before the bone became dust, the process stopped. Organs appeared in the ribcage. Muscle, and tendons and skin formed, and before we knew it, there was a new person lying on the table."

"Sarah Roswell," Fox and I say together.

I slump back in my chair. I'd been on the edge of my seat, leaned close to the table, but knowing the whole story sinks me like a grave. That's why Burgess was going to say Sarah wasn't his daughter. She's his wife.

And Sarah was born with the life force of my parents. Has she looked exactly the same for the past forty years? I wonder if she's a Quasi-Immortal, too.

"How did you end up stuck in a cell for a half century?" Fox's words draw me out of my stupor.

"I didn't trust Mr. Burgess, you see. With transactions like those, it's always best to be protected. They didn't call me the best Mage in the world for nothing, darlin'. I reworked the spell as I was casting it, kept some of the life force for myself."

"You made yourself immortal?" There are equal parts astonishment and disgust in Fox's voice.

What Bartholomew claims to have done is unheard of. I've been around a long time and privy to lots of Quasi-Immortal speculation and magical tinkering, but I've never even seen a spell that powerful, let alone know someone willing to 'rework' one.

"Yup. The old bastard tried every way he could to kill me. When he couldn't do it, he gave up and had me locked away. Those anti-magic cells are a bugger. I'm so glad you came along." Bartholomew stands up from the table.

"Wait, where are you going?" Fox rises, fists balled.

"I gave you all the information you wanted. We're even now. I'm going to go enjoy my newfound freedom."

171

Necrotown: Mountain City Chronicles

The knife is still in my hand. The knife is heavy. The weight of the blade carries it forward. The sharp metal slides into Bartholomew's chest with ease. The knife is still cold. Bartholomew's blood is warm. What doesn't kill you still hurts like a motherfucker. One of these days, I'll figure out how to kill that bastard, but right now I've got a bone to pick with Burgess.

Chapter 18

Crazy shit happens in the Glow all the time. It's the ghetto. A shithole. Maximus dumpimuss, if you speak Latin. Things like shootings, beatings, stabbings, and angry mobs happen often enough that residents of the Glow have just learned to keep their heads down and ignore all the shit. If you don't look crazy in the eye, it can't hurt you. Gaze averted, cross the street, stay out of everyone else's bullshit. That's about the only thing I like about the Glow—being left the hell alone.

Downtown, however, is home to lots of Standards who live very standard lives. Safe, sane Standards are not used to seeing dickhead Mages getting stabbed in a café. A dozen of those 'sane' shocked citizens are standing, staring at the knife sticking out of Bartholomew's chest. Half of them already have phones pressed up to their ears. The other half are staring in gape-jawed shock.

"Whoa, whoa, whoa," Fox yells and holds up her arms. "Just an act, everyone. We are just practicing for a performance at the concert hall next weekend. See?" She rips the knife out of Bartholomew's chest.

Blood spurts out of the open wound, soaking the white tablecloth of our table.

The Mage yells and presses his hand against the open wound. The hole seals up and the blood flow stops within seconds. Bartholomew moves his hand to show everyone the healed wound. "Yup," he says, jaw clenched. "All just an act. Carry on."

Good ol' Bart needs police attention even less than we do.

"You can catch us Friday night, staring in the new play, *The Mage Who Couldn't Die*. Now take a bow, gentlemen." Fox takes my hand and tugs me into a forward bend with her.

Bartholomew gives a hesitant bow, and we split for the door. Fox dips and grabs the duffel bag out from under the table, and I drop a twenty on it as we pass.

She leads me down an alley between the coffee shop and a barber, putting distance between us, the jailhouse, and the cafe.

"I assume that makes us even, and there will be no more retribution, Mr. Flint?" the Mage asks.

I spin, fists balled. "You carved…" I take a deep breath. "You took a blade and cut my parents for god knows how long, carving out a spell that took their lives. I have spent the last forty years wondering what happened to them, and now I find out a piece of shit Mage killed them to save some spoiled goddamn Standard? No, we are very far from even." My voice shakes, eyes burn.

"You can't kill me." Bartholomew straightens his tie and squares off his stance.

"Nothing is truly immortal, Mr. Gorstein. You, of all people, should know that."

The magician's hands glow with a blue aura.

"But today, I have bigger fish to fry. Kingpin first, lackeys later."

"What if I want to settle this now?" The blue blaze of energy increases.

Power draws from all around. Bartholomew is good, and being locked away from his power hasn't diminished his ability. I reach into the bag on Fox's shoulder and pull out the insanely large pistol. "How is this for settling things?" I squeeze the trigger.

The world goes silent before ringing stings my ears like a hornets' nest. I blink a couple times to refocus my vision. My ears won't stop buzzing. I press my hands against them. The gun is hot against my face. When I finally shake the cobwebs out, I focus on Bartholomew. The Mage is on the ground, grasping at the stump where his left leg used to be. Blood pools underneath his body, staining the blacktop. Within moments, the flow stops and the wound heals, but Bartholomew's leg shows no signs of regrowing.

I glance at the spells etched into the barrel of the gun. Those magic scribbles must really work. I aim at Bartholomew's head. A Standard cop car comes to a stop at the end of the alley, probably coming to investigate the cannon that just went off in Downtown Mountain City.

Fuck.

Fox grabs my hand, and we sprint down the alley in the opposite direction, leaving Bart clutching his stump of a leg. We cut across a city block then down and back in the other direction. By the time we stop running, we are near the Glow. A border of town houses divides southern Downtown and northern Glow. The town houses hold medium-income Standards. Secretaries, paralegals, assistants, and girlfriends all take up residence in a place that's still technically Downtown, but close enough to the Glow that no one with any money would live here.

There's a four-story apartment building in front of us. We circle to the back, and I grab the fire escape. The roof seems like the safest place to regroup, right? It's got a good view of the city, anyway. We can see if anyone followed us.

At the top, we check the stairs. No one. I rush to the front side of the building and peer down. No squadron of cop cars. Considering I blew a guy's leg off, I would have expected a slightly bigger response. "Do you find it odd the cops haven't chased us?"

"Let's not question a good thing." Fox drops the artillery bag.

"We should probably hang out for a little while. At least until the heat dies down."

"Come here." Fox calls me hither with her finger.

When I get within a step, she jumps out and wraps her arms and legs around me, latching on like a hungry octopus. I can't help but laugh. "What the hell are you doing, woman?"

She presses her cheek against my ear. "I thought you might need this." She nuzzles against my neck, and the feeling is like morphine. "You okay?"

"Yeah." I walk us over to a piece of heater or electrical or something and take a seat, keeping Fox in my lap.

"Don't lie to me."

"I'm a little fucked up."

Fox looks at me with a pained expression, her features softening. "Yeah. I can understand that. You were going to kill Bartholomew." It's not a question. It's not a judgment. "What can I do?" She squeezes my ribs tight.

"Nothing. Everything." I stare at her and press my face into her collarbone. Her heartbeat is a lullaby singing to my broken heart. What can I say? I just found out my parents were tortured and murdered over Lloyd Burgess and Sarah Roswell.

"Let's kill them both," Fox says. Dead serious. I know she means it with every ounce of her being, and that is more heartbreakingly beautiful than I can ever describe. There is no greater love than one willing to commit murder for you.

I bury my face harder against her chest. The image of my parents, my mother, hanging upside down over that pit in Necrotown, won't go away. I wasn't even there, and I can't shake seeing it as if I was. Blood covering their bodies, draining into that pit next to the throne of skeletons Sarah sat upon not even two days ago.

My head nods on autopilot. Yes, they will pay for what they've done.

We sit in a silent embrace for what feels like a momentary eternity. One single moment that's never going to end until suddenly it's gone. Fox kisses the top of my head and pushes herself out of my lap. "Stay here."

She digs through the duffel bag and comes out with a pack of cigarettes. She lights them both and passes me one. "So, who's first? Burgess or Roswell?"

I take a long drag, and the nicotine levels me out a little. "Before we get to the revenge killings, can I ask you a question, darling?"

Fox drops back into my lap and kisses my cheek. "Anything."

"Why didn't we get the car, instead of running four blocks?"

"Oh." Fox stands up, puffs a few breaths of cancer. "Well, we were trying to get clear of the cop, and the parking garage was in the other direction."

"And the blood on your neck back at the café?"

"You said you wanted to ask a question, not questions." Fox winks at me. It's sexy as hell, but it won't get her out of the trouble she's in at the moment. She's got some splaining to do.

"Fox. The blood?"

"Umm...cut myself shaving?"

I bite back a laugh. Impossible to look stern when I'm laughing. "And may I ask why you were carrying the bag of guns from the trunk?"

"No, you may not ask."

"Okay, no questions. I'll just talk, you can tell me if I'm wrong. I'm thinking you went back for that Hair kid. The blood on your neck probably came from one of the guards, all of whom are dead, if I had to guess. I would also wager we didn't go pick up the car because you gave it to that kid to get away in, and that explains why you carried our bag of tricks instead of leaving it in the trunk."

"That's a very interesting theory." Fox flicks her cigarette off the top of the building.

"How close am I?"

"Very." Fox bounces over and plops herself back in my lap again.

I lean back and rest on my elbows, staring up at my gorgeous wife, the woman who saved me. The view is stunning.

"That's why you're such a good detective." She leans in and kisses me on the lips.

"Fox—"

She kisses me again, harder. More.

"You killed—"

She bites my bottom lip.

"The cops are going—"

She parts my lips with hers. Her hips rotate, pressing against me, as her tongue touches mine.

I can't stop the moan in my throat. "…to be looking for the ones who murdered their own." I sit up and slide my hands up her back.

Her nails rake my chest, scratching through my shirt. "They will look at the footage," she says between kisses. "They will see one disgruntled guard kill the other two. The footage will show what looks like the guard shooting the Hair and dragging his body out from the station."

Fox wraps her fingers around my throat, pushing my head to the side. She kisses my neck, whispering in my ear. "The disgruntled guard made his way to a parking lot before he took his own life."

She bites my ear. My hands wrap around her hips and press her harder against me. "Fox—"

"They were corrupt."

"Fox..." my voice can't work above a whisper anymore.

"You saw what they did to that kid. They would have killed him."

"Fox?"

"What?" She leans away from me, her blue eyes wide with exasperation.

"I don't give one single damn about what you did back there." I stand, still holding her in my arms, and spin, laying her on her back. Her breath catches as I press against her. "I *need* you. Now, more than I ever have in any of my lives. I need you."

Our lips meet and Fox reaches for my belt. Desire boils off of her body. It makes me want her even more. Fox has seen me, she's seen my flaws and my shortcomings and my insanity. All that, and she still loves me. I need to be inside her, not inside her body, inside her soul. I need to be a part of her so she can never leave me.

"Am I interrupting anything?"

"Holy shit." I jump up, off of Fox, caught in the act on an apartment roof like some horny teenager. "Sorry about that, we, uh..." I turn to face our accuser and stare into the face of the last person in the world I want to see. I angle my body toward the menagerie of weapons only a few feet away.

Sarah Roswell swipes her arm through the air and the bag slides ten feet away from my grasp.

179

"The fuck do you want?" Fox is crouched low to the ground, an animal ready to strike.

"I came for you, brother," she eyes me. "It's high time we talked."

"I'm not your brother, and you should leave before I kill you."

Sarah laughs. She clicks her tongue, and two Mages climb up the ladder and onto the roof. These aren't run-of-the-mill, clown Necros either. These are full-fledged mercs like Burgess uses.

"We were both born of the same parents. I think of us as siblings. Or at the very least like a yin and yang. Light and dark. Life," Sarah points at me, "and Death," she points a thumb at herself. "Two sides of the same coin, if you will."

"We are nothing alike." I square my shoulders.

"No, we aren't. We are complete opposites. That's what I'm trying to tell you, but you know what happens when you combine the power of immortal life and immortal death? I'll tell you, baby, we can have the world. Come with me, and I'll show you."

"Fuck you, bitch." Fox growls. "He's not going anywhere with you."

"Please?" Sarah holds a hand out.

I can't stop the mirthless laugh from coming out of my throat. "No." The word is as cold and dead as Sarah as it rolls off my lips.

Sarah takes a band off her wrist and ties her long black hair back. "So be it. We'll do this the hard way."

The two Mages break for Fox, and Sarah charges me. Fox dives across the roof toward the bag. I glimpse steel, longer than a knife, but I can't see what it is. Sarah is on me in a flash. She shoves me back with a strength I wouldn't imagine. Strength bolstered by magic. Magicians never play fair.

I trip backwards toward the edge of the roof. Power swirls in the air as Sarah and the two mercs draw on the local energy pool. I try to siphon off a little for myself, but Sarah's draw is too strong.

One of the Mages screams.

Go Foxy baby.

Sarah charges again. Ready this time, I drop to a knee at the last second and plant a punch in her gut. She 'oofs' and takes a half step back before looking at me as if for the first time. "I was beginning to wonder if you had any fight in you at all."

I would kill for that magic gun right now.

A particularly large wave of magic whooshes by me like a sea swept breeze, only instead of salt and fish, this one reeks of death and dirt.

Fox cries out.

I try to look behind Sarah to see if Fox is okay. Bad idea. Before I can get a focus on Fox, Sarah has closed the distance.

The cold feeling of a knife drawing across skin is something I'll never forget. I've felt the kiss of a blade more than once in my many lives. It doesn't hurt, not at first anyway. Instead, it's more of a concentrated cold followed immediately by a warm rush of blood.

Sarah's blade isn't normal. There isn't a cold feeling. There is pain, more pain than I can remember. Like a serrated sheet of death. My throat burns like acid and fire and hell. The pain stretches from ear to ear. I suck air in through the hole in my throat. I taste blood at the back of my tongue. Sarah kicks me in the chest, sending me tumbling over the edge of the roof, and all I can think as I fall is, 'Is Fox okay?'

Necrotown: Mountain City Chronicles

Fox has to be okay.

Chapter 19

Shit.

I'm conscious, but body-less. This rebirth needs to hurry the fuck up so I can find out what happened to Fox. I swear if Sarah and her goons have done anything to my wife, I'll tear them to pieces.

Rebirth has always seemed like its own process, and I've never put much effort into making it faster, but right now, I need a body. I don't give a damn what happens to that body after I find out about Fox. She needs to be okay. If she's hurt because of me. If she's dead because of me...

Come on.

Come on, come on, com'on.

The familiarity of home surrounds my being. Great, mind is in place. Hurry up Quasi-Immortal ju-ju and give me appendages.

The pain is fierce as my body mends itself together out of the magic in the air. I have to focus. Where will Fox be?

Dead.

Fuck whatever part of my mind that came from. Some dark recess that houses my inner asshole.

Your inner honesty. Face it, she's dead. Those Mages were heavy hitters and that's without Sarah's help.

Muscles lace over my skeletal frame.

"Ff-fuck, you," I scream from my half-formed body.

Necrotown: Mountain City Chronicles

Skin. I need skin. I need skin and a ride. Soon as this is over I'm hauling ass straight to Necrotown. Sarah will be there. She will have answers.

Every fiber of my being warps with pain as the rebirth process completes. I drop to the floor, naked and shaking. I scream. The floor shakes under me. Get yourself together, Sam. My muscles squeeze with full effort. I slam my fist on the floor and force my eyes open.

There is a pair of sneakers in front of my eyes. Blood is smeared across the white rubber toe of the Chucks. The shoes are attached to feet. The feet are attached to legs. The legs are bound to a chair.

"The fuck?" I blink, trying to understand what's going on. How is Fox here? Why are her legs tied to a chair?

With all the focus and concentration in my body, I turn my head so I can look into her eyes. I see her lips move, but my ears aren't working yet. Whatever's going on, I've got to move. The floorboards bow as I push myself up.

Fox's eyes go mile-wide. Her mouth opens in what has to be a scream, and she shakes her head back and forth. She bucks and strains against the ropes.

My ears snap back into working condition just in time to hear the snap. The crackle of my spinal cord hits my ears a moment before pain sears through my body. My body is broken backward by a force. I try to fight it, but can't. When the magic releases its grip, my body collapses on its side.

Fox's chair scoots across the floor, bouncing against the wood. I want to look into her eyes and say everything is okay, but I can't. My neck won't turn. My arms won't respond. My legs are long past gone. This isn't the end of the world. All I have to do is die, and I'll be reborn good as new.

"K-ki-kill me," I force the words out.

Magic did the work of paralyzing me. A size thirteen boot does the job of snapping my neck completely.

Goddamn Mages. Or Sarah. Whoever it was.

How were they there? In my home? No one knows where I am reborn. Fox, but she wouldn't give that up. She would die first. How did they know?

Come on. Body. Presto. Magic. I need to get back there.

I've never died in my own birthplace. My mind is already in place and Quasi magic immediately starts rebuilding my body. Good. I need to get back to myself, figure out what's going on.

Bones fuse from nothing. The pain is a distant thought. What do they want? Sarah said something about joining her. So why kill me?

She's just trying to make a point. All she's trying to do is prove that she can kill me any time.

My body burns with what feels like a trillion volts. The shock hurts. It always hurts, but the pain is muted, muted by fear. How are we going to get out of this?

Same as before, magic finishes its work and drops my newly reborn body on the floor. I keep the scream on the inside. There's an audience, after all. Fox can't see me hurt. She has to know I'm all right.

My jaw stays clenched to bite back on the pain. I force my eyes open on those same bloodstained sneakers. Before I can open my mouth to say a word, a blast pops my ears. My head snaps forward and sprays blood across Fox's jeans.

I'm once again fucking dead. What's these guys' deal? Is this some kind of Quasi-Immortal trickery like Bartholomew killed my parents with? This doesn't feel like special magic. It just feels like they are trying to kill me. To actually kill me. I'm defenseless. At first birth, I can barely stand, let alone fight off two Mages and a supreme Necro.

Maybe this is it. Maybe this is the end of Sam Flint. Wouldn't be the worst way to go, I suppose. Shotgun blast to the back of the head or snapped neck or whatever does it. I wonder if they are switching methods to keep from getting bored. Hopefully the next one doesn't involve water. Drowning is my least favorite way to die.

What about Fox?

That stupid voice. Fox is fine. Once I'm dead, they'll probably let her go.

If that's the case, why is she here?

I have to get back.

Staying alive long enough to get answers would be nice.

At least I'm not *dead*, dead yet. Wonder how many do-overs I have left.

Mind becomes bone becomes nerves becomes muscle becomes skin. Human once more. I don't even open my eyes before I roll toward Fox's chair. Hopefully she hasn't moved.

My chest bumps against her legs. She's closer than I thought. Maybe she has scooted her chair closer in her struggles. No one has blown my brains out yet, so that's one start in my favor. I reach out and grab hold of Fox's pants. Ignoring three deaths worth of pain, I pull myself up and rest my head in her lap. Her stomach heaves against my face as she takes deep, unsteady breaths.

"...come on, Sam. I need you to get it together, baby. I need you to fight back for me right now."

I open my mouth and my jaw moves, but no words come out.

"You can do it. I believe in you. I need you to believe in yourself, Sam."

With both palms against her knees, I shove up and off and hope to end up on my feet. My legs hold. I force my eyes open. Fox forces a smile. She's covered in blood. My blood. She nods her head, encouraging me to get my shit together and kick some ass. Her gaze flicks over my shoulder and just that quick her disposition drops.

There's no time to turn or fight before a cord slips over my head and around my throat. My windpipe closes, and I gag. I try to slide my fingers under the garrote, but it's too tight. Whoever is doing the choking is taller than me, and the cord is pulled tight. My weak legs give out from under me. The attacker holds strong, suspending me by the rope around my neck.

Fox screams. Tears roll down her face. She thrashes against her binds in the chair until it falls to the side and makes a splintering sound as it hits the ground. She ups her struggle. Muscles thick as cords bulge from her neck as she screams louder.

The corners of my vision fade to black. I reach behind me. Maybe I can get a grip on the attacker, but it's no use. There's no strength left in my body, and my hands slap limply against the side of the attacker's face. I'm lowered to the ground without the cord loosening, until I'm face to face with Fox, our noses almost touching.

Her eyes are wide. Tears of pain and anger roll off her face as she stares at me. I can't do anything, too weak to fight back. I'm hurting Fox, letting her down. She has worked so hard to save me, and I can't even fight off one Mage to save myself. My arms whip around one last time, trying to do anything to stop the attack. I open my mouth to scream, but no sound escapes the squeeze of the rope.

She wails a sound I've never heard a person make before. I can taste her tears on my lips. The cord tightens around my throat and blackness closes. I try to keep my eyes on her, but my vision goes out, and it clicks in my mind that Fox is screaming my name as everything fades away.

Necrotown: Mountain City Chronicles

Chapter 20

I'm still alive. Or at least I think I am. My mind is still here. I just need another body. Again. The look of pain on Fox's face before I died is the only thing I see. Her eyes solid red from crying. The agony in her voice as she screamed my name. Fox needed me, and I failed her.

She told me she needed me. She begged me to get up and help, and I wasn't strong enough.

A tingle starts at the base of my feet as my skeleton rebuilds itself. What's it even fucking matter? It's not like I'll be able to do anything other than die and die again. I'm not strong enough.

Stop being a bitch.

My inner voice sounds a lot more like Fox than usual.

You can fucking do this. You can take these assholes. I know you can.

Fox?

That's me.

Is that actually you?

In the flesh. Or, at least in the mind.

How?

You reached out for my hand before you died. It seemed like a good chance to hitch a ride.

Muscles thread themselves across my body.

You can't stay Fox. I don't know what will happen if I die and don't come back while you're with me.

Necrotown: Mountain City Chronicles

I will die with you, as the happiest woman alive. But that's not going to happen because you can beat this. I know you can beat this.

I'm sorry, Fox. I'm not strong enough. These guys are killing me before I can even get my feet under me. They are stronger and better in a fair fight, and this is anything but fair.

Bullshit. That same power that's coursing through Sarah is in you, too. Just stop being afraid.

I'll try.

No. You won't try. You fucking will.

Okay, I will, but make me a promise.

Anything.

As soon as I'm conscious again, get back in your body. I can't risk dying with you riding along like this.

Silence. Just the distant pain of my femoral artery snaking its way down my inner thigh.

Fox?

Fine. I'll go back, but you better not die.

Deal.

The skin finishes sealing up my body. I reach out, and my hand brushes Fox's arm. The bastards didn't even bother moving her. She's still tied to the chair lying on its side. My skin tingles as Sune travels across my arm and back home where she belongs.

With Fox safe, or as safe as she can be, I let go. Fear of death. Fear of failure. Fear of life. Everything that's been weighing on me for as long as I can remember, I let it go.

I take a deep breath and taste the magic in the air. The magic in my home. *My* magic. As I reach for it, the energy seems to recede into the depths of the house, like I'm not allowed to touch it. I have to focus, this is *my* home, *my* magic, *my* power. The energy swells in the room, slowly coming to me. I draw the power into my chest, and use it to bolster my muscles. Like hitting the boost button on a racing game, my body bursts to life. I push off the floor and almost fly backwards.

Power moves through the room, swirling behind me as one of the Mages tries to siphon off the energy for himself. I turn around and find the merc with a blue orb glowing in his hand. The orb is pure power, probably enough to kill a man. My mind opens to the house. I can feel every part of it. It's amazing. I've never felt this before. This has been my home my entire life, and until this moment, it was just a place. Now it's a living, breathing thing full of life and energy.

The same energy the Mage is gathering in his palm. With a mental snap, I push more energy into the orb. The Mage looks confused for a second as the ball grows. I overload the Mage. The juice is too much. The orb explodes in his hand. Explode is a bad word for what happens. It's not like a grenade or a land-mine or an a-bomb even.

The 'explosion' is silent. The energy just expands and in a snap, contracts back to nothing. Only, when it contracts it takes the left two-thirds of the Mage's body with it. The Mage's one remaining eye goes wide as a fist before his body—one arm, one leg, and half a ribcage—collapse to the floor.

"What the?" The second Mage comes running out of the kitchen, apparently confused by the lack of me being dead.

"I'm going to tear you apart, you son of a..."

The wooden beam overhead drops and cracks the Mage in the head. For all the power Mages have, they aren't durable worth a damn. The magician falls to the floor clutching at the back of his skull.

"Fox?" I ask.

"Yeah?" I don't even have to look to know she is still struggling against the ropes holding her to the chair.

"How exactly did this asshole kill me?"

"He's the one that choked you to death, honey."

I walk over to the still writhing Mage. He has his face to the ground and doesn't even seem to notice me approach. I kick him in the ribs to help him roll onto his back. The merc, all special agent slick a few minutes ago, has turned into jelly. He's whimpering and sobbing.

"Please, I'm sorry. It was just a job. Sh-she made me do it." Snot pours out of his nose and mixes with tears and spit running down his face.

I plant my knee in the center of his chest. He used a rope, but I don't need one. Ten fingers work just as well. My hands wrap around his neck, and my thumbs press against his throat. I can feel his windpipe crushing beneath my fingers.

The Mage gurgles and hacks. Around me, energy swirls as he tries to call it to him. This is my fucking house. My power. I keep all the juice for myself and squeeze harder. The guy's eyes bulge wide before his struggle ends the same as his life.

I stand up off the dead Mage.

Behind me, someone claps. I turn to find Sarah Roswell seated in a chair in the corner. There's no telling how long she's been there.

"I wondered how many tries it would take before you found some balls. I was beginning to think you wouldn't make it, but I must say..." Sarah's eyes scan my naked body top to bottom, "Very impressive."

Behind me, Fox's chair snaps.

Alexander Nader

Chapter 21

Fox dusts pieces of broken chair off herself and comes to stand between Sarah and me. Her fists ball. My wife is one intimidating lady, but this isn't a fight I'm willing to risk her life on. I reach out and set a hand on her shoulder. She shrugs it off and plants her feet.

"Cute," Sarah says, eyeing Fox. "But my business is with your husband." She swipes a hand through the air. A chair slides across the floor and crashes into the back of Fox's knees, forcing her into the seat. Black wisps of energy wrap around her wrists and ankles, restraining her.

"If you're trying to get on my good side, hurting my wife isn't the way to do it." I siphon some power, just a small amount. Maybe if I build it up little by little, Sarah won't notice. The energy tastes like home. There's no other description for it—just the smell I've known my whole life. The smell of my clothes, of my bed, of *my* house.

"She's not hurt, just out of the way. Right, honey?"

Fox's eyes close to slits, and her face burns red. Muscles in her arms flex as she strains against the black magic holding her in place.

Sarah strolls across the living room and into the dining area. The table had four wooden chairs, carved from trees around my home. One chair is broken to pieces and covered in my blood. Sarah takes another one away from the table and has a seat. Crossing one skinny jean-clad leg over the other, she leans back in her chair like hanging out with a naked Immortal and a furious Kitsune is how she spends her Tuesday afternoons.

"It's about time you showed some potential," Sarah says, her gaze roaming over my body again. "Do you know how long I've been waiting for you to stop being such a whiney piece of shit?" She nods at the scars on my forearms. "Almost forty years." She tilts her chair so it's resting on the back two legs. "Our parents gave us so much."

My blood boils. "Call them our parents again, I'll kill you."

Sarah coos, "Touchy touchy. I meant no offense."

"No offense?" The muscles in my chest are strung tight enough to snap. "You had my parents killed to save your pathetic life."

"Not me. Lloyd." She shrugs. "He had all of it done without my knowledge. He did this to me," Sarah twirls a fine black mist of magic with her hand, "and he killed your parents."

"You expect me to believe you had no idea what was going on?" I keep siphoning power from the room at a trickle. Energy swells inside my throat and tingles at the back of my mouth like I swallowed an Alka Seltzer.

Sarah sits forward in her chair, hands on her knees, lip curled. "Have you ever seen someone with stage four cancer? Have you seen the treatments? Chemo, doctors, more chemo, radiation, more doctors, meetings about experimental drugs, feeling like walking death, *looking* like walking death? It's a never-ending cycle of misery. I was dead from the day they told me I had six months left to live. The time frame was just a formality. Believe whatever you want, Mr. Flint, but I am telling you I had no idea Lloyd would do what he did."

She doesn't look like she's lying. I glance at Fox, hoping for a second opinion. She is a missile of rage aimed in Sarah's direction. Put in her position, I can't blame her. I couldn't bear to watch anyone mess with Fox the way Sarah is messing with me right now.

"We can't change the past, but we can talk about the future. Which is why we've come together today." Sarah leans further forward in her seat. "Now that you've tapped into your potential, how much power *do* you have?"

I give her a blank stare.

"Don't play me for dumb, Sam. I know you've been pulling at the magic in the room."

So much for the element of surprise. I extend the least amount of energy I can toward the dresser in the corner of my living room. Orange strings of light open the drawers and bring a ripped pair of jeans, stained t-shirt, briefs, and pair of boots to me. I dress myself without taking my gaze off Sarah. "Just needed to build up enough juice for a change of clothes," I say.

"Cute parlor trick, but you used nothing on that. So you do have some gusto in there."

I crouch to tie my shoes. "I suppose."

"Always denying what's inside you. Such a shame. You know I put this together for you?" Sarah spreads her arms out wide, gesturing to my gore covered house.

"You had two assholes kill him repeatedly for his own good?" Fox's teeth clench so tight, I'm not even sure she could get any more words past them.

"Absolutely. Sam has been pathetic for a long time—just a ball of depression and self-loathing, a waste of power. You see, I've been keeping tabs on him since I came back. I needed him to discover his talents, but he just kept on his downward spiral. Until he met you, that is." Sarah pouts at Fox.

Fox strains harder against her binds, but Sarah's magic is too strong. I might be able to break the constraints, but even two on one, I'm not sure I like our chances against the Necro. There's a time to fight and a time to listen. Now is the time to listen. If Sarah wanted me dead, I would probably be dead.

"I still don't see what she saw in you," Sarah goes on, "a puddle of slit wrists and empty whiskey bottles. But whatever it is, she changed you. I watched as you started to give a damn, dressed nicer, died less. It is truly impressive what a good woman can do for a worthless man. She built you up to be something better than yourself.

"Then I pushed you. I challenged you to be something greater. To find your power." Sarah pushes to her feet and crosses the room toward me. She looks up into my eyes. There's a look in hers, adoration maybe? Not in the sense of desire, but in the way a parent looks at a child. "I helped you harness the energy you were born to wield. I *made* you."

"Thanks." My forced smile feels more like a grimace.

She scoffs. "Don't you know how *hard* I worked for this? Do you know how difficult it was to find this place?" Sarah scans the room. "*Your* parents worked hard to hide your birthplace. Do you know I can speak to the dead? They tell me things, help me find things. But this place?" She points at the floor. "There isn't a single dead body within 30 miles of here. Not one dead person in all of time. *That* is impressive."

"So you had to actually do some work to find my home? Good for you."

Sarah's nostrils flair—a brief flash of anger. "Do you know how much work it took to wait on you to find a backbone?" Her voice pitches higher.

I may have just poked the hornet's nest. With all the delicacy I can muster, I reach my energy out toward Fox's binds. Sarah's magic is tough, but as she likes to keep reminding me, the opposite of death is life.

"Finding out you were in debt to the Trolls wasn't hard. Paying them off to kill you was even easier, especially with Lloyd's bank account to draw from. I made sure they killed you in front of the fox." Sarah angles her head back at Fox without looking over her shoulder. Good thing because Fox's restraints are rapidly dissolving.

"I knew Fox would hurry back to you. I originally planned to follow her, but she was nice enough to take along the Troll that killed you. Knowing the two of you and your knack for vengeance, I thought I knew where things were heading. Sure enough, you killed the Troll, and I had a dead body inside Flint Manor."

"Well-played." I'd clap, but it's taking all of my focus to work on Fox's restraints. She's got one leg free. "So what do you want? What's the end game?"

"Power, of course. After I came back, I immersed myself in the grimoire that held the spells Lloyd used to bring me back. I found quite the interesting spell inside there. As it turns out, if immortal death and immortal life combine, it makes for a very special duo."

"What does that even mean?"

"I want you to combine your life force with mine. Our power will become fused." Sarah reaches out for my hand. I step back, away from her.

Both of Fox's legs are free.

"What do you want with all that power? You are already the most powerful Mage I've ever seen."

Sarah touches her hand to her sternum. Her youthful features go soft. "Aww, thank you. That's sweet. But it's not enough. I want to run this city."

"You already do," I say.

"No, Lloyd runs this city, and he is doing a terrible job of it. Look at the Glow. All the money in the world, and he lets a huge portion of the city fall into ruin. And this war with the werewolves? Petty."

"So you're going to war with Burgess, and that will be better?"

"That's why I need you, Sam." She reaches out for my hand again. I step back again. Sarah winces. "If I tried to take out Burgess now, with all his money and the Mages of Mountain City under his thumb, it would be a bloodbath. But, if we combine our power? No one would resist. I could take over with minimum lives lost, and I could save this city."

"Minimum lives lost?" I've got one of Fox's arms free.

"Lloyd would have to die, of course."

"You'd kill your husband to take over the city?"

"Oh, please." Sarah shakes her head. "Lloyd Burgess possesses things. He owns everything, and he thinks he owns me. Why do you think he hired you when I dropped off the radar? He needs to possess me like I am actually his daughter or one of his merc Mages or his slave or something. I mean as little to Lloyd as he does to me. Did you know he married me because my parents were rich?"

"Um, no?"

"Lloyd built his empire on my parents' investments. Believe it or not, that liver-spotted old man was young and charming once, and I thought he wanted me for me. It only took five years of marriage and a couple multi-million dollar business contracts before he told me he married me for money. What was I supposed to do then? Admit that it was a sham?"

"So instead you pretended to be the good wife for fifty years until you could take him out?"

"Why not? He used me. The door swings both ways."

"And why would *I* help you with your quest to take over the city?"

"Because I can give you what you want."

"And what do I want?"

"Peace," Sarah says. A brown leather backpack slides across the floor and stops at my feet. The bag opens to reveal more cash than I've seen, ever. Sarah didn't even have to wave a hand for the magic. "This is for you. Take your lovely wife, take the money, and split for the beach. I hear St. Augustine is lovely this time of year.

The Trolls have been paid, and I will take care of Burgess—you are free and clear."

Oh.

That's not a deal I was prepared for. I've wanted to disappear with Fox forever. That was even our plan when this was all over. Take the money and run. My power would be tied with Sarah, but it's not like anyone could mess with her. Hell, no one could fuck with me. A chance at just Fox, me, and the beach.

I dissolve the last bit of magic holding Fox to the chair.

"Come, join us, Mrs. Flint." Sarah waves a hand. No magic attached, just a come hither motion.

Fox stands and takes up place beside me.

"I have something to return to you, Fox." Sarah never takes her gaze off me, apparently unfazed by Fox being free of the Necro magic.

A katana with an orange sheath and brown leather handle floats in front us. Fox reaches out a hand and takes the blade. It's the same one she picked up from Ethan's, I think. She slides the sword a couple inches out from the sheath. The metal blade shines with an orange sheen. She slides it back.

"What do you say?" Sarah holds out a hand.

What do I do? Make a deal with the devil? She wants to save the city, or at least that's what she says. This crazy-ass spell might not even work. Then again, it worked with my parents. All I want is to be alone with Fox. This is our chance. Our chance to be us. Just us. I don't like Burgess, I don't even like this city.

I kiss the side of Fox's head, whisper in her ear, "What would Foxy do?"

She grabs the side of my face and kisses me hard on the lips—her mouth tastes like blood. "Just you and me, babe. Let's find us a nice little spot in the middle of nowhere."

"Fine," I say. "I'm in. What do we do?"

Sarah smiles. "What else, brother? We die together."

Chapter 22

"Excuse me?" I say.

"You heard me right, we die together."

"Can you even die?"

Sarah nods. "We combine our blood, and we die together."

"Uh-huh," I say. "As long as you go first." My palms sweat. This is the right thing to do.

I think.

Sarah sighs. "There's two of you. *You* go first."

"Fuck that." I pace a couple steps. I'm not killing myself again. How many lives has Sarah cost me? And I'm going to lose another one? Fox catches my hand as I pace by to stop me. This is worth it. For me, for her, for *us*. Calm down, Sam. Hell, I've cut my own wrists before, this isn't different. I'll come back. I always come back for her.

Fox turns to me and takes a deep breath. She mouths, "You sure?"

I nod, hold my arm out.

Fox draws her blade down my arm delicate as a lover's touch. The blade is sharp enough it doesn't require pressure to cut through flesh, muscle, and arteries. There is no pain, only blood.

Sarah holds her arm out, and pulls up the sleeve of her shirt. She looks at Fox and then at her own wrist.

"After the stunt you just pulled, finding Sam's power or not, it would be a pleasure." Fox's eyes are still red from crying. She makes a twelve-inch incision down Sarah's arm.

Sarah doesn't even flinch as the blood flows. She takes hold of my arm, close to my elbow, pressing our flesh together. Something in the air changes. That power, the energy of my home, that familiar taste of everything I've always known, turns up like a volume knob cranked all the way to the right. The energy builds even as my skin grows cold and my light fades. Sarah and I collapse to the floor simultaneously.

I'm dead, a spirit, and then I'm not. My body fuses together in record speed. I'm whole again with no pain and in no time.

Fox is in a chair with the sword laid across her lap. As soon as I'm back she stands. "How are you?"

"I'm…" I have always felt the inherent energy in the air, and after Sarah's stunt, I could even play with the energy, but now, now I feel like I *am* the energy. Power buzzes around me like I could just disappear into the air and ride the waves to wherever I wanted. Maybe I can. "I feel great."

I grab my last bit of clothing out of my dresser and get dressed. Sarah's body stitches itself together out of thin air in the middle of my living room. I've never seen what it looks like when a Quasi-Immortal is reborn. The process is hard to watch, knowing how painful each step is, but there's a kind of beauty to something born out of nothing.

Sarah's rebirth completes, and the energy drops her to the ground, naked and shaking. She screams in pain, and a tear rolls down her cheek.

Good. I'm glad that hurt.

It takes a few minutes for her to catch her breath and extend out of the fetal position. "My god, that hurts," she says when she finally manages to get to her feet. "Would you mind?" Sarah looks at my shirt and down at her body.

I take my shirt off and throw it at her.

"Thank you." She tugs the shirt on, covering herself.

"Are we done here?" Fox wraps an arm around me and starts for the door.

"Don't forget your loot," Sarah says.

The brown leather bag of money slides across the floor and stops in front of our feet. I bend and scoop the bag up without breaking stride. "Thanks."

"No, brother, thank you. I'll be keeping an eye out on you. I hope you'll do the same for me."

"Why is that?" I ask.

"Because, it's not just our power that's tied together now, it's our lives. If I die, you die. And that's a permanent thing, if I read the spells right."

Great. Just fucking great. This is what happens when you deal with the devil, you get burned on the details. Whatever.

I grab the door and yank it open, revealing one very angry, one-legged Mage reaching for the handle. Blue balls of energy crackle in his hands as he punches me in the chest with both fists.

Chapter 23

A magically charged punch to the chest feels exactly as good as it sounds. Okay, that's an exaggeration. The punch hurts, and my back slamming into the stone fireplace after being launched across the room is what really puts the pain receptors on notice.

Fox draws her sword in a flash. An orange glint shines as her blade slices out at Bartholomew with vicious speed. The energy in the room dips as the Mage tops his tank off and uses the power for a boost of speed. His form blurs as he slides across the floor, not even seeming to move his lower body. He's fast, but not as fast as Fox's blade. Her katana cuts off at least three of Bart's fingers as he slips to her left.

Bartholomew probably thinks he's being smart, moving away from Fox's dominant hand. She's better than that. Before one-leg has even stopped to retaliate, she has switched the sword to her left hand and sliced back again. The Mage screams and covers his chest with his arm. A bloody gash stretches from shoulder to hip, but the cut isn't deep enough to cause any real damage. Mages are just worthless when it comes to dealing with pain.

A huge surge of energy moves through the house like an invisible tidal wave heading straight for Bart. He's pulling hard, and I'm not about to hang out while he blasts it all at my wife. It's been fun watching Fox kick his ass, but this fight is over. I stop the magic before it can get to the Mage. Just to add insult to injury, I siphon some of Bartholomew's own energy back out of him. The magic tastes like coffee grounds and stale bread.

Once I have what I think is enough energy—I guess it's enough, I'm new at this whole magic thing, either way, it feels like a lot—I focus the surge into an orange ball, crackling like lightning in a bottle. With a mental heave, I push the ball across the room. Bartholomew turns as the projectile reaches him and absorbs it into his chest without a flinch.

"Impressive," he says, "but we were born of the same magic. You'll have to try harder than that, Flint."

My parents, hanging upside down and covered in blood, flash before my eyes. I see it this time. Actually see it. Through the Mage's eyes. I don't know how. Maybe he's sharing it with me, maybe I'm taking it, but either way, I'm looking directly into the horror this son of a bitch inflicted on my family, my blood.

We may have been born of the same magic, but I've just made my crossroads deal with Mephistopheles. Time to see if this new magic is all it's cracked up to be.

I open my mind up to the room. The power, *my* power, swells in my chest like a breath of air. I let my mind go, pulling on the thread I worked at earlier. In a moment, I've ridden the wave of power across my house, disappearing and reappearing just in front of the Mage.

Bartholomew's eyes swell. That's as much time as I allow him to react. Sarah is still in the room, probably watching to see what I do. I don't have to see her to feel her imprint on the atmosphere. Her magic, Death's magic, tastes like cemetery dirt, but I don't care. I've got a point to make. I suck in the macabre energy like the dregs of a whiskey bottle.

My energy, Life energy, feels like swallowing an Alka Seltzer tablet. Sarah's is that feeling when you're alone in the dark, but suddenly you don't feel so alone. Those pinpricks that run down your spine.

I jab my hands forward, plunging my fingers into Bartholomew's chest. With a heave, I rip my hands apart, splitting the Mage down the middle. Plasma and organs and shattered ribs fall to the floor at my feet.

Blood drips from my hands. I flick them off trying to dry them. Sarah and Fox are staring at me, both gape-jawed. The leather bag full of money is still at Fox's feet, close to the front door. I take

Fox by the hand, draw the bag to my fist without even having to borrow any extra energy, and make for the door.

"You know, you could stay. We could rule the city together," Sarah says.

"Fuck you," I say.

"I wasn't talking to you."

I freeze. Both Fox and I turn over our shoulders to look at Sarah.

"What, Fox? I like you." Sarah leans up next to my fireplace, elbow propped up on the mantel. "You've got passion and fire. You are a woman of action. Together, we could fix this town and show these people what real women are capable of."

"I...what? You tied me to a chair." Fox says.

"You weren't listening. Better than what I did to him." She nods in my direction.

"And where do I fit in your scheme?" I ask.

"Have you heard the saying, 'behind every great man is a great woman'?" Sarah smiles.

"Yes."

"Well, behind every great woman is a decent guy with enough power to rip the city apart and who takes orders well. For her," Sarah eyes Fox, "I think you'd be just that guy."

"No," Fox says. She reaches for the door.

"Think of how great it would be to rule. You could have it all. We, the three of us, could be like gods." Sarah snaps her fingers. The fireplace roars to life with black flames.

Fox opens the door. "We just want to be left in peace. Have fun ruling the city. I'm sure you will find plenty to join your crusade, or whatever."

Sarah holds her hands out to the fire, a smug grin on her face. "Fine, but you take care, Mr. and Mrs. Flint. Our lives depend on it."

"Right." I kick the door closed behind me.

Chapter 24

The sun has almost completely set behind the mountains, casting an orange glow through the woods at my house. My magic is orange, everything about Fox is orange—a good sign. I hope.

"Holy shit, Sam, did you just rip a man in half?" Fox sheaths her sword and follows beside me.

"It would seem that way."

Parked out front is a Mountain City Police cruiser and a large, black SUV. I'm guessing the cop car came from Bartholomew and the SUV goes to Sarah. Sarah can deal with getting home in a stolen cop car. I get in the driver seat of the SUV.

There's no key, but that's not enough to stop me. A little mental sweet-talking has the engine running and ready to go by the time Fox is in the passenger seat. I turn around and start down the driveway.

"Something really changed in you, didn't it?" Fox's head is tilted forward, actual concern clear on her face.

"Yeah, I think so."

"You have power now, *lots* of power, but you're still...still the same, right?"

I smile at Fox, lean over in my seat and kiss her on the lips. "Still the guy you married. Promise."

Fox smiles, kisses me back. "So this is it, then? We take our bag of money and make a run for the beach?"

"I was thinking less of a run and more of a leisurely cruise down the coast. We just keep driving until something tells us to stop."

"That sounds nice, but you better put your eyes on the road."

I've driven this driveway enough times to do it blindfolded. Using magic to hold the wheel, I take her face in my bloody hands and kiss her forehead. Two red handprints mar her cheeks when I remove my hands.

Fox laughs. "Cute trick, but hands on the wheel. I think I might be married to the most powerful man alive, and I'd like some time to enjoy that before painting the forest with our bodies 'cause you couldn't keep your eyes on the road."

"Fair enough." I take the wheel back and wink at her. She just called me the most powerful man alive. A fella could get used to talk like that. I try to keep the asshole grin off my face.

"You're grinning like an asshole."

"You just called me the most powerful man alive."

"If the shoe fits... Just try not to get too cocky about it."

"I'll try to contain myself."

"You don't feel bad? You know, about leaving the city with," Fox glances over her shoulder like she's checking to make sure Sarah isn't in the back seat, "with her?"

"Mountain City is a shit hole, yeah?"

Fox nods.

"Sarah wants to change the city. How much worse could it get?" I shrug. "Who knows, maybe in a couple months, we'll be sitting in a hammock, drinking mojitos and reading about how Sarah Roswell saved the city."

"Maybe." Fox leans back in her seat and props her feet up on the dash. She's still covered in my blood. Hopefully that's something she'll never have to be again.

"Did I make the right call? Do you want to go back with Sarah?" I always just assumed Fox wanted what I want. Maybe she does want to live like a goddess. She deserves it.

Fox takes my hand in hers. "It means you and I can be alone, in peace. I would damn the world to have nothing but you. Samuel Flint, you are all I need. Forever."

"Let's hope I didn't just damn the world."

"You know what I meant." Fox slaps the back of my hand.

I turn off the dirt path and onto the main road, point the car southeast. We can be at the water before dawn. Fox turns up the radio and leans against my shoulder. She moans, and the sound sends shivers down to my soul.

This is it. We can have everything. Just her and me and nothing else. The scenery doesn't even matter. Maybe the beach will suck. Maybe we can get lost in the woods somewhere. Just camp out for all of eternity. The choices don't matter, what matters is we have a choice.

Something swells inside me, something I haven't felt in a very long time. It's not magic. It's not pride. It's hope. With our hands knotted together, Sune strolls down Fox's arm to brush against my fingers and I can feel her soul touching mine. I kiss the top of her head, and pray for a clean slate when that sun comes up tomorrow.

*****End*****

Made in the USA
Columbia, SC
05 February 2024

31005754R00126